Threads

Threads

5/2/15
mike & Genera
Hope you like my
first novel!
Mary Wright

Mary Howard Wright

Library of Congress Control Number: 2014916188
ISBN: Hardcover   978-1-4990-7105-4
                 Softcover   978-1-4990-7106-1
                 eBook   978-1-4990-7107-8

Scripture quotations are from the Holy Bible, King James Version (Authorized Version). First published in 1611. Quoted from the KJV Classic Reference Bible, Copyright © 1983 by The Zondervan Corporation.

Except for scripture quotations marked TNIV are taken from the *Holy Bible, Today's New International Version®. TNIV®* Copyright © 2001, 2005 by International Bible Society®. Used by permission of Zondervan. All rights reserved worldwide.

Author's photograph and the image of the cover work of art provided by April Amodeo of Amodeo Photography. Used with permission. Original art for cover is titled, "Home is Where My Heart Resides" and was created in October 2008 by Marie Collier. Used with permission.

This book was printed in the United States of America.

Rev. date: 10/03/2014

To order additional copies of this book, contact:
Xlibris LLC
1-888-795-4274
www.Xlibris.com
Orders@Xlibris.com
657976

CONTENTS

"You are never too old to set another goal

or to dream a new dream."

- *C. S. Lewis*

My heartfelt gratitude to the following folks for their support in the writing of my first novel: Dan Smith, author of "Clog!" for his technical assistance; Jamie Rand, VT for his insightful and gracious copy edit work; fellow authors - Charles Lytton & Sally Campbell Repass for their advice and expertise; Judith Joness for her help in identifying just the right scripture for each chapter; Kathy Hurt Marshall for her help with medical information; Marie Collier, local artist, for the painting, "Home is Where My Heart Resides," painted October 2008 which graces the cover; April Amodeo of Amodeo Photography for my personal photo and her photo of the cover art used for the cover; and of course, all my family and friends who were a continuous source of love, support, encouragement. A special nod to my parents, who would put on a pot of coffee and listen eagerly as I read the "hot off the press" chapters to them. It was a joy to see how my literary creation could evoke emotions, stir sentiments and create dialog. I hope you enjoy this first book in the Tapestry Series.

CHAPTER 1

First Love

Many waters cannot quench love, nor can the floods drown it. If a man would give for love all the wealth of his house, it would be utterly despised.

Song of Solomon 8:7

Fletcher, a man with strong Christian values, was deeply in love with his wife, Rachel. Theirs was an unfolding love story. Every major decision in his life since meeting her had been made thinking how best to honor God and their marriage. He was so enamored with his wife that he couldn't remember the significance of his life before her or imagine living without her.

Unlike some men, ambition and success in life were not the all consuming fire that stoked him. What kindled his spirit was his family and wanting what was best for them. The last few years, 1919-1921, had been especially challenging. The outside world seemed intent on doing its best to drive a wedge between them.

His mind drifted back to the first time he saw her. Rachel's family moved to the little German hamlet where Fletcher had lived all his life. Her father came seeking work with his own small family in tow.

They settled into the little house behind the smithy. Rachel's father, Amos, was an older gentleman with kindly eyes. Fletcher rarely saw Rachel's mother, Katherine. He occasionally spotted her sitting on their front stoop and noticed her sallow appearance. Sallow. It was the word his mother had used to describe her.

He didn't know what sort of health problem Katherine had. She rarely came to any church meetings. Truth of the matter was, if not for her attractive daughter, he probably wouldn't have noticed her at all. He thought that was probably a sad commentary on the preoccupation of a young man's mind, but truthful, however shallow. He'd once asked Old Doctor Smyth about Katherine, and he'd replied she had something called "consumption." Little was known about that disease around these parts.

Rachel carried much of the housework load as she shopped and cooked for the family. She was mature beyond her years and worry showed in her eyes. His mother said Rachel had an "old soul." He wasn't sure what that meant, because when he looked at Rachel, he saw only youthful beauty, in perhaps its rarest form.

When her family moved here, it was the summer of his nineteenth birthday. Rachel was three years younger. He, and of course every other eligible young man in town, took notice of the new neighbor with the big brown eyes, pert little nose, long curly hair and sassy attitude. Apparently, she wasn't the least bit interested in any of the young men trying their best to catch her eye or steal her heart.

Fletcher naturally attributed her personality to her parents spoiling her and never having to share their attention. He noticed that the other girls in town eyed her suspiciously, not wanting the competition, he thought. They had nothing to fear, since Rachel rebuffed all attempts by fellows trying to get to know her better.

Her parents must have either married late in life or had their first child in their later years, because they were considerably older than his parents. Her gray-haired father was a quiet man with a trim beard and moustache that curled up at the ends. He was extremely adept at his trade of both making horse shoes and shoeing horses. He quickly found work at the local blacksmith shop with Mr. Kerr. Together, they made both a nice team and a reasonable living by providing a respectable and much needed service for their community.

When Fletcher came in that afternoon to wash up, his mother, Hilda, told him about running into that nice Anderson girl at the market that morning.

"Why haven't you been by to talk to her yet, Fletcher?" she asked.

Rubbing his hands through his hair, Fletcher met his mother's gaze. "Well, it could have something to do with the fact that she doesn't seem at all interested in me, or anyone else for that matter. There are plenty of other girls I can talk to."

His mother quietly studied her youngest son for a moment. "You can't fool me," she said. "I see you watching this girl. I know you think a mother doesn't notice things, but you are wrong. Your dear old mom doesn't miss much. And, what's more, I saw her watching you in church last week."

She had loved the shocked look on her son's face. Yes, a little motherly meddling might be in order here. His older brother, Peter, had married his childhood sweetheart, Karen, as quickly as they could get permission. Fletcher, however, had never been serious about any of the girls in town.

Maybe he was just waiting for the right one, his mother mused. She thought she had the perfect one in mind for him. Now, to figure out how to get those two stubborn people interested in each other. Her husband warned her to stay out of it, because it certainly was not any of her business. Of course, his mother had other ideas.

Fletcher's mother planned a special meal for the Sunday of his nineteenth birthday. She went out of her way to call on her new neighbors, Amos and Katherine, and of course, Rachel. She invited them to join her family after church that next Sunday. At first, they resisted, but no one could thwart his mother when she got her mind set on something.

Rachel's parents agreed provided Hilda let Katherine bake a cake for the occasion. His mother hesitated because she had always baked his birthday cakes. She quickly agreed and Katherine welcomed a chance to get her young daughter out of the house doing something fun, for a change.

Rachel protested that she didn't have anything suitable to wear to a birthday party and didn't know what sort of gift might be appropriate. When she got home from the market the next day, she found a beautiful blue dress with an ivory silk ribbon belt lying across her bed. Her mother had sewn the dress for her.

Katherine originally wanted to give the dress to her daughter for Christmas that year, but this was the perfect occasion. And, of course, she was anxious to see her daughter's eyes light up in surprise. Really, to be such a young lady, Rachel was far too serious. Her young life was not an easy one taking care of her sick Momma. Finally it was settled. They were going.

Her father purchased a fine pocket knife that he told her any young man, or old one too, for that matter, would love to possess.

Fletcher's mother really outdid herself in preparing his birthday feast. She had cooked up one of their favorite cabbage and corn beef dishes along with fresh garden carrots, onions, potatoes and some homemade yeast rolls. She certainly pulled out all the stops to try to get the two of them in the same house and sitting down for a meal.

As it turned out, only Rachel and her father had shown up for dinner. Katherine was having some breathing problems and Doctor Smyth forbade her to leave her bed. Rachel wanted to cancel too and stay with her mother, but Katherine and her father insisted that they go and not disappoint his mother. Fletcher thought, *Bless Katherine's heart for pushing them out the door that day with his birthday cake in hand.*

His parents greeted them at the door. "Amos," his mother said. "It's so good to see you and Rachel, but for heaven's sake, where is Katherine?"

In his quiet manner, Amos quickly made an apology for Katherine's absence. Fletcher didn't miss the worried look on his face. When they stepped into the room, he got his first full look at Rachel. Her suntanned face glowed, her eyes sparkled and she couldn't possibly look any more beautiful. She wore the dress her mother made for her. Fletcher thought she looked like a princess. Of course, his mother arranged for them to be seated right next to each other at the small table. They all sat pretty much shoulder to shoulder. He noticed that his mother didn't remove the extra chair that was for Katherine.

Awkwardly, Fletcher was at a loss for what to talk with Rachel about, but luckily, the adults carried the conversation. He and Rachel exchanged embarrassed smiles and shy glances throughout the meal.

After dinner, they enjoyed the wonderful chocolate cake Katherine baked and iced so fancily for his birthday. His parents, always practical, gave him a nice new leather belt which he definitely needed. Amos offered their small gift. Fletcher carefully untied the ribbon and undid the simple wrapper. He couldn't believe the great little knife they got for him. Amos had expertly carved Fletcher's initials on the wooden handle to both Fletcher's and Rachel's surprise. Amos hadn't even mentioned it to her.

Fletcher's parents and Amos took their coffee and went out to the front porch to visit. How like his mother to figure out a way to leave them alone. Rachel got up and began to clear the table. "Shall we take care of the dishes for your Mother? It seems like the least we can do after that delicious meal she prepared for us."

Fletcher had never washed a dish in his life and couldn't think of any reason to start now. "I don't really think my mother expects you to do the dishes, you are our guest. And I know she wouldn't want me doing dishes on my birthday," he told her playfully. "Would you like to go for a walk instead? We can go out to the orchard and see if the apples are getting ripe yet? I have some fencing my father keeps asking me to check on down that way, too."

Not the smoothest way to get her to take a walk with him, he thought. But it would be good to get away from the parents so they could talk and get to know each other better. Glancing at her, he thought she looked like a scared little bird. Maybe God gave him just the right words to make her feel at ease.

She flashed him a radiant smile and he felt his heart beat faster. When she said his name, it beat faster still. "Sure, Fletcher. It's a beautiful day. Let me tell my father where we are going and make sure it's alright with him."

Her father was enjoying the chat with Fletcher's parents. He waved the young couple on. *My daughter is growing up*, he thought. *I have been so busy with my job and her mother's health problems, that I have gone unaware that she has really become quite a lovely young lady now.* It was the first time, as a father, that he had really thought that there would come a day when she would be leaving them and going out on her own.

Would this be the young man for her? He certainly seemed like a nice enough fellow and Amos already liked the boy's family. He rubbed his head and took a deep breath. Where had the years gone?

The young couple were walking down the road towards the apple orchard when Fletcher asked, "Rachel, do you mind if I ask you about your mother? I don't want to pry, so it's alright if you'd rather not talk about it."

Rachel's face tensed and he noticed tears glistening in her eyes.

"Oh, Rachel, please don't cry. I am sorry to be such a stupid clod. Please forgive me for asking you such a personal question. It really is none of my business and you don't have to answer."

Fletcher wished the ground would open up and swallow him whole. How could he be such an idiot? Here he was, out alone with this beautiful creature and really, this was the best he could come up with as a conversation starter? He thanked his lucky stars that she hadn't taken off running in the opposite direction. He was sure she thought his inquisitiveness bordered on rudeness. She had every right to tell him so too.

"Fletcher, may we sit for a moment?" Rachel asked.

He removed his vest and smoothed it out on the grassy knoll. He couldn't help but notice how stunning she looked sitting there. He hoped she didn't ruin that pretty new dress.

"Every day I worry about my mother's health," Rachel said. "I don't really see any overall improvement, but some days she seems to brighten. Then, within a few hours, her strength seems to drain away.

I do what I can to help her. Sometimes, I feel so selfish for wanting just a normal life like other girls my age."

She glanced sideways at him expecting him to be totally judgmental and shocked at how horrible she was. Instead, she saw understanding in his eyes.

"Rachel, I think you are magnificent and I can't even imagine the patience and love it must take to give of yourself daily to care for your mother."

"Thank you," she said.

"Your mother must be a saint," Fletcher said. "I see her at church and out occasionally. Never have I heard one complaint from her lips. I think some of the folks in town would be willing to help if they knew how to do it without making matters worse or offending your family."

"My parents are very proud and aren't accustomed to asking for help," Rachel told him. "They would be mortified if they thought people in this community felt sorry for them." She shrugged, as if trying to shake off the hurt. "We manage. My father has taken her to different doctors but none of them has been able to come up with a remedy for her condition."

He nodded, not knowing what to say, and she went on. "I guess I have accepted that she may not be with us for very long. That alone makes every moment I have to spend with her so dear to me. She is not a burden, but she does worry about being one. I don't know how I can make her understand that Father and I love her so much. We don't resent her, but we do wish by some miracle, she could be cured and be able to have a more full life."

"I understand," he said.

Rachel looked at Fletcher. "Do you mind if we head back?" she asked. "We can come see the orchard another day."

He smiled. "Sure," he said. "Is that a promise?"

When she nodded he sprang to his feet and offered his hand. Hers felt small and soft in his rough ones. He decided in that moment that there would never be another girl for him. Her eyes met his and he swore he saw something light up in them. He continued to hold her hand as they walked along. She never pulled her own away.

His parents were inside and her father had gone home by the time Fletcher and Rachel returned to his house. His parents had assured Amos that they would make sure Rachel got home safely.

Fletcher and Rachel nervously unclasped hands as they approached his house, but not before his mother, looking through the kitchen window, had noticed them. "Quick, John," she whispered. "Come over here and see for yourself."

He came to the window and peered out. After a moment he said, "Don't you go reading too much into their new friendship. She is very young."

"Just listen to you! Do you remember how young I was when you asked me to marry you? And how young I was when we got married? I was just fifteen when we became engaged, sixteen when we got married and not quite seventeen when the good Lord blessed us with your first son!"

Her weary husband shook his head. He knew when he was in a losing battle. When that woman got something in her mind, there was no convincing her otherwise. He knew she was already imagining who their first grandchild would look like! A man had to accept when his opinion didn't matter, there was no getting around it, that's just the way it was.

They stopped at his house and retrieved her mother's cake dish. Fletcher walked Rachel home. They made plans for him to come by her house the next afternoon when her father got home. Fletcher had volunteered not only his own, but his father's help, with some of the work that needed to be done around her house.

She was concerned that her father would be reluctant to accept their help, but he certainly could use it. Knowing her dad, he would barter with them and offer to shoe their horses or something. He wouldn't want to feel obligated or for them to feel like his family was taking advantage of their kindness. But yes, with the long hours he kept and his care responsibilities with his wife's condition, he could use not only the help but the friendship, too.

They parted at her doorstep with another set of parents looking through the living room window at the romantic drama that was unfolding before their eyes.

"Oh Amos, I think our little girl is falling in love. He seems like such a sincere young man. What do you think of him?" Katherine asked her husband.

"I like him." Amos grinned. "He's sweet on her alright. Let's see what our girl thinks of him."

CHAPTER 2

Wedding Bells

Therefore shall a man leave his father and his mother, and shall cleave unto his wife: and they shall be one flesh.

Genesis 2:24

Weeks turned into months and the months into a year. Fletcher could hardly wait to wake up and find an excuse to see her. At first the fathers both worked together with Fletcher, then just her father and Fletcher, then finally Fletcher alone as the list of chores dwindled. Her parents' house and lot had received a much-needed facelift. In between trimming trees, sanding chipped paint, and planting flowers, Fletcher and Rachel had fallen deeply in love.

There were the awkward, stolen looks at each other at first, as he worked about the house and yard. Sometimes, she daydreamed and stared out the window while she washed the supper dishes. Often, while standing there, she saw Fletcher heading down her family's path with a rake or some other tool in hand, grinning from ear to ear and whistling a happy tune. Her heart would leap at the sight of him. There were the special times together after she got her mother settled in from her evening meal when Rachel would come and sit on the front steps with him. They talked while he worked.

Many an evening, they sat together and talked until dark about everything and nothing. They wove a future together without realizing it at the time. Just one more thing in common, one more shared experience, a longer look into each other's eyes which words didn't interrupt. It wasn't long before this was all repeated while holding hands, sitting just a little closer together or with Rachel softly leaning in against his strong shoulder. He felt like heaven and earth was right there in her eyes. His heart was lying at her feet so vulnerable was he to her. He was so nervous the first time he put his arm around her, but it just felt so right.

He would never forget their first tender kiss. He had held her like she was a fine china doll and gently tilted her chin up to align their lips. Her lips, so soft and warm, tasted like the sweetest honey. Neither of them had closed their eyes that first time, although he heard that was how it was done. He didn't want to take his eyes off her for even that split second.

Nervously, she said, "Fletcher, I think I'd better get inside."

He knew he never wanted to be apart from her. Yes, his father and brother teased him unmercifully about the little brown haired girl down the lane.

"What else could possibly need to be done over there at her place?" his dad had wondered aloud with a wink at his mother.

Fletcher always had a list of chores that he needed to finish over there before winter.

His Dad said, "Well, just let me know if you need mine or your brother's help."

"No, I can take care of the work," Fletcher said. "It's not hard, just time consuming."

One evening, he went by the blacksmith's shop and talked with Amos. He asked her father's permission to marry Rachel. Amos told him he would be proud to have him as a son. Fletcher swore him to secrecy. He needed that time to work up his nerve to ask Rachel if she would have him.

He didn't say anything to his parents. It was too special to risk his dad teasing him about it. He wasn't sure his mom could keep that big a secret. There was no doubt in his heart or mind that Rachel was the girl for him. She stole his heart the first instance he had seen her.

Amos went home that evening and gently broke the news to Katherine. He didn't want her to have too big of a shock when the proposal came. Katherine cried happy tears and promised not to say a word to their daughter or anyone else for that matter.

On August 9, 1913, at his twentieth birthday dinner at his family's house, this time with Amos, Katherine and Rachel all present, Fletcher asked the love of his life to marry him.

He got down on one knee and said simply, "Rachel, I love you, will you marry me?"

They hadn't talked of marriage; but Rachel's heart felt like soft butter when she looked down into his loving eyes staring up at her.

"Oh Fletcher, Yes, yes I will!" she exclaimed.

From his pocket, he took out a small golden, oval shaped, black onyx ring with a minute diamond chip in the center.

"Rachel, this is the best I can do for now," he apologized.

She thought it was the most beautiful ring she had ever seen. "Oh Fletcher, its perfect!" Rachel said through teary eyes.

Fletcher just didn't know how to take those tears. He hoped she wasn't disappointed. Girls were so hard to understand, but she looked happy despite the tears.

For a long moment, he was unaware of anyone else in the room except Rachel and himself as he straightened and took her in his arms. As he looked about the room, he noticed his mother and hers hugging each other, their eyes brimming with tears and happy smiles. What was it with women and tears?

The proud fathers came around the table, pounded him on the back and congratulated him. His Dad gave him a big hug and Fletcher couldn't be certain, but he thought he saw a tear in his dad's eye too.

They planned a November wedding. It was to be a simple affair with just the immediate family, small church congregation and the minister present. They planned to get married in the church where he had toddled up the aisles chasing after his older brother when he was just a couple of years old. He had so many memories of growing up in that church.

When Amos got up that morning of her wedding day, he took his steaming cup of coffee and walked out onto the porch to survey the skies. Rachel had just gotten up from her bed and heard the front door close softly. She threw on her coat and went out to stand on the porch with her father.

Her mother had a rough night the evening before with her cough and was still having difficulty breathing. Rachel had slept fitfully, listening for her mother's breathing to regulate. She made a poultice and placed it on her mother's chest. Finally, she seemed to get some relief.

"Rachel, my dear," he started, "I do believe we are going to get some snow today. Perhaps you and Fletcher should postpone your wedding plans."

"Oh Daddy," she laughed, "a little snow won't hurt anything. Besides, we are all set. The only thing left to do is for you and me to pick up the flowers and take them by the church. Maybe, it won't snow after all."

After she prepared their breakfast and cleaned the kitchen, Rachel took her bath. She pushed her long auburn hair up into an attractive up-do hairstyle. Gently, she placed the lovely white rhinestone combs on either side of her head. Fletcher gave them to her as a wedding gift yesterday while they were out on a romantic walk in the woods. She didn't buy him a wedding gift. He would just have to be satisfied with the gift of her undying love for him today, she laughed softly.

Her parents sacrificed and bought a lovely strand of pearls for Rachel to wear on her wedding day. Her fingers felt the cold, smooth orbs so carefully knotted with the delicate clasp. She gently placed them around her neck. They gleamed softly in the lamplight and the late morning light filtering through her laced bedroom curtains.

Rachel's mother insisted on making her simple, but elegant wedding gown. The empire waistline and beaded bodice perfectly set off her womanly shape. She used some of the lace from the dress and carefully stitched the cutout lace roses onto the sheer netting of her veil. Each rose was painstakingly beaded around the edges and in the center. The gown and veil were exquisite. Maybe, someday she would have a daughter who would want to wear her mother's wedding gown, she mused.

Rachel bundled up her mother and the two of them headed into town. The pretty color of her gown actually seemed to bring a bloom to her mother's cheeks. Even so, Rachel couldn't help but notice how frail her mother appeared. She worried about her traveling on this cold day.

Her mother admired her only child. "Rachel, my dear, your father and I are so proud of you and the beautiful young lady you have become. You are beautiful through and through and we love you with all of our heart," she said. Her voice was barely above a whisper and it came with a labored breath.

Rachel hugged her mom. "Thank you for all that you did to make this day so special. I shall treasure this memory forever!"

When they reached the market to pick up the flowers, a light snow had begun to fall. They covered the flowers with a soft old blanket hoping that they would not get crushed before they reached the church.

"Oh Dad, you jinxed us with all your talk of snow this morning, you old dear!" Rachel exclaimed.

By the time they arrived back at the church with the flowers, the sun shone brilliantly. Church ladies helped gather the flowers and place them where they needed to go in the beautiful old building.

Rachel thought her groom was so handsome standing up in front of the church watching his bride walk down the aisle. They had the most poignant service, not long, but just right. There was hardly a dry eye in the building. The wedding party left the church and went back to Fletcher's house where the neighbors had gathered to feed the family and the young married couple.

A nice fire was blazing in the fireplace and Rachel's mother was seated close by. Rachel would never forget the happy expression on her mother's face that day or the loving way her father watched his own bride.

And, so their life together began, ever so simply and sweetly. No one could take their eyes off the handsome young groom and his extraordinarily lovely bride.

CHAPTER 3

Love Grows

And may the Lord make you increase and abound in love to one another and to all, just as we do to you,

1 Thessalonians 3:12

As newlyweds, they lived with Fletcher's parents and stayed in his old bedroom until their home was ready some three months later. His parents' house had an upstairs with two small bedrooms that had belonged to Fletcher and his brother, Peter. It was a convenient arrangement, but every young couple craves a place to call their own. They immediately set about looking for something they could afford.

The home they found was not the storybook one they imagined as their first home. It was deserted and in poor repair when they bought it. But, from the front porch, you could see and hear a bold stream trickling over ancient stones and see the most amazing sunrises. Despite its dilapidated condition, it spoke to them. The property had nearly five acres of gently rolling land with majestic trees and a long rutted path leading to the front doorstep.

Beginning early in the morning and throughout the day, Fletcher worked in his Dad's or neighbor's fields. They needed to save nearly every cent so they could afford to buy their home. Soon, he had enough to work out a payment arrangement with the widow who owned the property. She was in ill health and living with her family in the next little hamlet. It turned out to be a blessing for both her and them.

When he and Rachel went to talk with the lady, her eyes had misted over as she looked at the young couple. In their eyes, she saw such sweet love; it reminded her of her own story in that house.

She told them, "I don't know if you are getting such a bargain. They tell me, the old place has fallen into such a state of disrepair now. When my husband and I first married we built the house. Almost immediately, we discovered that we were expecting our first child. That really put a fire under our efforts." She laughed. "We managed to celebrate our first Christmas in the new home. I can still remember the smell of the new wood and the first fire my husband built in the fireplace. We just sat in front of that fire and fell asleep. Both of us were exhausted! In the spring of the year, we welcomed our first child, a son, in that house. Love grew our family as God blessed us with two more children, both little girls."

She wiped tears from her eyes. "I lost my husband at a young age. He was thirty-four. He was a soldier. I never remarried. I didn't have room in my heart for another man because I loved him so much. I raised our young family. Now that I've gotten older, they are taking care of me."

Rachel and Fletcher were holding hands. He squeezed hers, knowing she was on the verge of tears. They both noticed that the dear lady was still wearing her wedding band after all these years. It touched their hearts to see that tiny symbol of the couple's love.

After they had signed their paperwork with her, she hugged the young couple and wished them all the best. "I hope you will be as happy there as we were. He was the love of my life and those were truly the best years for us."

With all the legalities behind him, Fletcher began to work in earnest on the house. He was relieved to find it had a good well. He patched the roof, replaced and glazed broken windows, and cleaned out the rubble from the previous tenants. Rachel cleaned until her hands and muscles ached. She and her mother had selected fabric and made bright little curtains for the windows.

While Fletcher labored to reestablish the fencing and prepare the soil for his garden, Rachel washed and painted the dingy walls. Fletcher, along with his dad and brother, replaced bad boards in the front porch and enlarged it a little. Soon, the house took on a warm glow. It was finally ready for them to move in. They were able to get Fletcher's old bedroom suite from his parents and a kitchen table and chairs at a bargain price from a neighbor. Her father had given them a wardrobe. Peter and Karen gave them a small sofa. Rachel's parents gave them a matching pair of oil lamps. They could officially play house now.

That next year, on a frosty fall morning in October, Rachel gave birth to their first child, Joseph. She had an easy pregnancy and labor. He was a chubby little fellow with the sunniest disposition. Joseph had his paternal grandfather's hazel colored eyes with gold flecks which changed from brown to green in a twinkling with the slightest change in lighting.

He brought them so much joy. They loved to awaken to his sweet little cries. Rachel cuddled him close and looked into those big eyes. Someone told her that babies are born with adult size eyes. They looked enormous in his small round face. They delighted in every milestone as he grew from an infant to an active toddler.

He was definitely Daddy's little boy. Nothing made him happier than seeing his dad coming down the lane from a hard day's work. He ran down the path to meet him as fast as his little legs would carry him. Fletcher scooped him up in his arms and Joseph's small arms wrapped around his neck. He laid his curly head on his dad's big shoulder.

The grandparents loved playing with Joseph and spoiled him to no end. They took turns taking him home with them after church on Sunday. This was nice and gave the young couple a chance to spend some quiet time together as a couple. Sometimes they would pack a picnic lunch and Rachel would watch as Fletcher fished for their supper. Often, on a good day, he would catch enough to take his parents or Rachel's a nice batch for their dinner too. Sometimes, they foolishly used that time to work on a project around the house, like the flower beds or loading stones in the wheel barrow to clear the yard or fields.

Often, when they got by to pick up their little fellow, they would find him and the grandparents napping. They grinned and exchanged knowing looks. Trying to get Joseph down for his nap must have worn out Mama and Papa too.

When Joseph was about sixteen months old, Fletcher and Rachel discovered that they were expecting a second child. Rachel had a lot of trouble with morning sickness this time around. She wasn't one to lie around in bed in the morning, but she didn't seem to have a choice for the first hour or so. That was tough to do with an active little boy running around. Sometimes, Rachel was able to coax Joseph to climb in bed with her and look at his book. After a few months, the sickness finally subsided and she began to feel like herself again. She thought of friends of theirs who said they went through nausea with all their children. Once was enough as far as Rachel was concerned. She pitied them and hoped she didn't have to go through that anymore.

Once Rachel started feeling better and getting her energy back, she went more frequently to check on her mother. Lately something had changed with her.

To Rachel, her mother's smile seemed somewhat weaker, her recovery time from her bouts longer and her mother's old rallying energy seemed to have disappeared. She visited as often as she could, which was never as much as she liked. There always seemed to be one more job she had to get done at her own house. They were still somewhat a work in progress remedying the problems that came with owning an old house.

To help out, she started cooking her parents' meals. It was simply a matter of cooking a little more than she normally prepared for her own family. Rachel's dad was usually exhausted when he got home and yes, she noticed the worry in his eyes. When he came through the door every evening, the first thing he did was go into the bedroom to check on Katherine. As often as she could manage, Katherine waited for him in the living room. She could remember a time, when her Mom sat at the kitchen table with a cup of tea and read her Bible while waiting for her husband to come home.

With increasing frequency, she and little Joseph had to go into town to get old Doctor Smyth to make a house call for Katherine. Rachel was fairly experienced at recognizing what was normal and what was not, when it came to her mother.

As Doctor Smyth walked them home one day he told Rachel, "You know, you would make a good nurse if you were interested. You've done that job all your life, haven't you Rachel?"

"I had to, so Dad could work and support our family," Rachel said. "I worry that Momma is taking a turn for the worse. Is she?"

"Her body is weary. She has fought a good fight, but it takes its toll over time. I wish your folks lived near a big city, so that your father could consult with physicians much more specialized than I am. I am just a simple country doctor, you know."

"Is there a chance another doctor could prolong her life? Is there some special medicine or treatment that she needs? We will do anything we can."

The old doctor put a fatherly arm around her shoulders. "Rachel, I don't really know the answers to those questions. From my many years of experience, I do know that I'm looking at a patient who is nearing the end of her life."

Rachel burst into tears. It frightened Joseph who was walking by her side. He began to whimper too. She picked him up and held him close. "I'm so sorry," she said. "It's not your fault, but it hurts so much to hear."

"Here, here now. Do you remember in Ecclesiastes where the Bible says to everything there is a season? The good Lord had determined before we were born exactly what path our lives will take. For now, just continue to care for her, in her home. Be there when she needs you, just as you've always done, dear child. That will make her comfortable as possible until her time comes."

She nodded miserably.

"I need to tell you something, Rachel. Your father cannot accept that she won't get any better. I tried to gently prepare him for that eventuality. He loves her so intently that the message cannot get through. When that day comes, it is going to be the hardest thing in the world for him to deal with. He has been a good husband to your mother."

When Fletcher got home, that evening, she told him what the doctor had said. She could never hide anything important from him. Especially not now, here in the seventh month of her pregnancy, when her mood was so low.

"Rachel, this is hard, but you are going to need to be strong for your father. I'll be strong for you. I know you love your mother, but when the time comes, we will have to let her go." He took her hands in his. "We'll go through this together. I promise."

Rachel continued to go back and forth with meals and took the best care of her mother she knew how. Sometimes, that meant just sitting quietly and talking with her while she shared her memories. Katherine enjoyed having her grandson about the place with his boyish smile and sweet little kisses. Rachel sensed that her mother knew her time was close, but she didn't talk about it. Rachel didn't know what information Doctor Smyth had shared.

Time marched on and in no time, her new baby was clamoring to make his appearance in this world. When Rachel went into labor with her second child, the pain was so fierce, not anything like with her first child.

Fletcher tried his best to comfort her. Her labor started out intense so he only had time to get his mother's attention to go get the midwife. He found himself wishing he had brought his mother over to his house and went after the midwife himself. He was so worried about Rachel; he thought he should stay with her.

He carried in a cool pitcher of water to offer her a drink. When he reached out his hand to wipe her forehead, Rachel tried to bite him. The midwife, Mrs. Meyer, arrived along with Fletcher's mother just in time to witness the funny little scene. Mrs. Meyer ordered Fletcher out of the room and winked at his wife with a smile twitching on her lips.

This labor was more difficult than her first labor, but Rachel was a strong young lady with a great deal of fortitude. Soon, Joseph was joined by a red faced little brother, Arwood. The tiny little guy had a fiery personality. Where Joseph woke them with coos, Arwood came into the world screaming. From that first day, they knew that this little fellow might prove to be a challenge to their limited parenting skills.

Rachel's father came by her house to see the new grandson. He held the little guy and told Rachel that he was a beautiful child. Amos didn't stay long. He was anxious to get to his own house and check on her mother.

CHAPTER 4

Amos and Katherine

Yea, though I walk through the valley of the shadow of death, I will fear no evil; For You are with me; Your rod and Your staff, they comfort me.

Psalm 23:4

Riding home that dreary evening, Amos was excited to tell Katherine about their new grandson. She was in such good spirits that morning when he left. Actually, it had been the first time in a long while when he left for work without fretting too much about her.

Usually, when Amos was away, he would come home so they could have their lunch together. Today, however his journey had taken him farther out into the countryside. That morning, knowing he couldn't make it back in time for the meal, Amos packed some bread and cheese to take with him. Stopping by Rachel's house made him even later arriving home. Katherine always worried when he was late.

The first thing he noticed was that the house was so dark and quiet. There were no cooking aromas, no scent of hot coffee. Frightened, Amos rushed into their bedroom and found Katherine almost completely unresponsive. He spoke her name, touched her face and got no reaction. He suddenly found himself in a complete panic.

He bolted out the door in search of Doctor Smyth. He couldn't shake the deep sense of foreboding that filled him. When he reached the good doctor's house, his wife invited him inside. Amos stood there pitifully, holding his hat in his hands.

The poor man, thought Mrs. Smyth. He looked ashen. She offered him a cup of coffee which he refused and just stood there shifting nervously from foot to foot.

Her husband wasn't feeling well himself this evening, and after dinner, he had gone upstairs to his bath. He'd been hoping to turn in early. Mrs. Smyth climbed the stairs as quickly as her arthritic knees would carry her. She told the doctor that Amos was in the drawing room and looked worried to death.

The doctor rose from his comfortable chair where he had sat reading and enjoying his coffee. He quickly dressed and grabbed his weathered physician's bag. As they rushed back to the little cottage, Amos told him what he could about Katherine's condition.

Doctor Smyth looked sideways at him. Katherine's health had been rapidly declining in the last year, but Amos wasn't ever ready to face that fact. When they got to the house, the doctor rushed inside.

"Amos," he said, gently, "I know you are concerned about your wife, but please, wait here. I will come and get you as soon as I know something."

He quickly went to Katherine's bedside. She was not breathing. He did his best to resuscitate her. Finally, he gave her a shot to try to stimulate her heart. It was useless. Katherine's life was over. He stood there for a moment composing himself and thinking of the words to tell Amos. He hated this part of his job, but now it was his obligation to give this good man the awful news.

"I'm so sorry, my friend, but Katherine is gone. Her suffering has come to an end," he said. Amos let out a howl like an injured animal. The sound came from deep within him. He collapsed into a chair, his face in his hands, utterly lost in his misery.

Doctor Smyth let the news sink in for a moment. He went to him and placed his hand on Amos' shoulder in an effort to comfort him. "Amos, do you want me to go bring your daughter back to your house?"

"No," Amos said. He looked up at the doctor. "Thank you for your kind offer, but my daughter has just given birth. I don't think she is strong enough to come out. There is nothing she can do anyway."

He paused for a moment, and then went on. "I'll go by her house tomorrow morning and tell her. Would you mind stopping by the Pastor's house when you go home? Ask him to come and give Katherine his blessing and pray with me tomorrow morning?"

Smyth nodded silently and left. Amos sank onto the bed. His tears soaked the pillow where Katherine's sweet head rested. He didn't want to share her with anyone. He held her tightly in his arms and sobbed like a baby. Her flesh still held warmth.

She had died in her sleep. Her weak body had finally succumbed to the consumption that had plagued her for the better part of her adult life. Strangely, Katherine's lips curved in a peaceful smile. How could that be? Her life had never been easy. Even in death, it seemed like she was trying to let him know she was at peace.

Dear sweet Katherine, you know I love you. Thank you Katherine for bringing me so much happiness, for our lovely daughter. She has your looks and your caring heart for everyone around her. I'm sorry to be so selfish, but I don't know how I will be able to live without you by my side. How can I tell Rachel you're gone?

His mind pictured his only child gazing into the eyes of that precious new baby boy. She loved her mother with her whole heart and soul.

Amos fell asleep in the chair at his wife's side without a thought of supper.

Rising before dawn the next morning, he stretched his sore back and straightened his stiff legs. He lit the lantern and went into the kitchen to put on a pot of coffee. He felt hollow inside. Out of routine he scrambled an egg for himself and sliced a piece of bread from the loaf his wife made the day before. He felt like he would choke trying to eat.

He dreaded the business of telling folks about Katherine's death and helping get Katherine ready for the wake. He didn't know, for the life of him, how he would bear up under the complete feeling of helplessness he was experiencing. He'd never been responsible for all the details and decisions to be reached at the end of life. His parents' deaths were cared for by other family members. He didn't know where to begin and felt completely overwhelmed. His legs felt leaden as he hitched the horse to the wagon and prepared to go talk with his daughter.

Rachel didn't sleep very well last night. She arose early to have a few quiet moments to herself before the household woke up. Standing in her kitchen, looking out the window at the sunrise, she was surprised to see her father coming down the lane in his wagon.

The old dear, she thought. *He is coming to check on me. This is early even for him.* She slipped on her robe and slippers and went out on the porch to greet him.

"Daddy, I'm can't believe you came over here so early. You were just here last night. Are you worried about me? I'm fine. Fletcher is taking a little time off to help me with the children while I get back on my feet."

As he stepped down from the wagon, Rachel's heart nearly stopped at the stricken look on his face.

"Oh Daddy, what's wrong? Are you alright?" As soon as the words left her mouth, she knew deep down in her heart why her father was there that cold morning. Rachel sank down on the porch steps, momentarily immobilized, unwilling to comprehend.

Amos quickly crossed the little lawn, and held his daughter in his arms as he had done so many times years ago, a lifetime really, when she was his little girl. She cried her eyes out into her daddy's shoulder, soaking his shirt. He did his very best to contain his own grief. Rachel could feel his trembling and it made her keenly aware of his heartache.

"Let me just go inside and wake Fletcher," she said. "You wait here."

Her husband was sleeping soundly. He jolted awake when Rachel touched his face. Though drowsy, he saw her sad look and the tears streaming down her face. He didn't know what to think. The new baby kept them up most of the night.

Rachel sat down on the bed beside him and told him about her father's early morning visit. She shared the terrible news that he brought her. Fletcher held Rachel and gently stroked her hair as she sobbed softly, trying not to wake the children.

"Don't worry," he said. "When the children wake up, I'm going over and get Mama and Papa to come by to help you and Amos. They will know what to do. You just go see your mother now."

They both had known this day would come, but still, neither she nor her father was prepared for it.

Rachel and Amos embarked on the short ride back to her old home place. Neither spoke as the sunrise broke brilliantly in the eastern sky, coloring everything gold, orange and pink. The beauty took her breath away. She suddenly felt very grown up and very weary at the same time.

She was too young to be burying her mother. Her mother was too young to be gone. Tears streamed down her face when Rachel realized that Katherine didn't get to meet Arwood. Someone once told her that when one person dies another was born to take their place. That was not a kind or helpful thought today. Her mother would have loved this little boy.

They arrived at the house. Rachel quickly stepped down, rushed up the steps and into the house. Amos worried that this was all too much for her so soon after the birth of her baby.

He watched as their daughter smoothed her mother's hair and kissed her cool cheek. She fussed over Katherine, straightening her bed clothes one moment and holding her hand and stroking it the next. He had no idea what Rachel was saying to her mother, but she was softly whispering to her as if they were sharing some great secret. Her goodbye brought fresh tears to his eyes. He did his best to compose himself. After all, it was his job to be strong for his daughter right now.

Rachel raised the window and quietly closed the door to her parent's bedroom. She began bustling around the kitchen and living room tidying up. Amos begged her to sit. He worried about her being on her feet so long. But there was no convincing her. Perhaps she just needed to stay busy.

It startled them when they heard a brisk knock at the door. When Amos opened it, there stood Fletcher's parents. His papa told Amos to come and go with him to talk to the pastor so they could make plans for Katherine's burial arrangements. The two men left quietly, Rachel's father's feet beating a slow shuffle across the floor. Watching them leave, Fletcher's mother thought he looked horribly lost. She told Rachel that some women from the church were coming over to help. She guided Rachel by the elbow out the front door where

Fletcher's brother and sister-in-law were waiting to take her home. Rachel protested, but her mother-in-law was having none of it.

"We can handle this," she said. "We don't need you collapsing from exhaustion. You need to get back to your family and get your rest."

Rachel was too stricken to do anything but nod.

CHAPTER 5

Goodbye Little Milk Maid

To everything there is a season, A time for every purpose under heaven: A time to be born, And a time to die; A time to plant, And a time to pluck what is planted;

Ecclesiastes 3:1-2

That night, soft candles and lanterns flickered in every corner of the small cottage. Katherine lay in state, dressed in her finest gown made by her own hands. Her hair was gracefully brushed and styled with her favorite hair pin holding it back.

The house was clean, cleaner than it had been in years. The neighbors showed up with many enticing dishes and desserts. An old-fashioned wake was underway. It was called what it was because no one slept. They told stories and shared memories of the dearly deceased.

Amos found himself caught up in all the activities. He wasn't accustomed to having so much company. He barely had time to think before someone was prompting him to talk about Katherine. Oddly enough, he felt comfortable talking to these wonderful friends about his memories.

Rachel was sitting by the fireplace holding her newborn baby. She had never heard her father speak of his and her mother's romance. It never occurred to her to ask them how they met. Maybe she was more self absorbed than she realized. She sat spellbound like everyone else present, listening to her father speak of his love and their childhood.

He described his wife as a "little milk maid." She had been about thirteen and he had been seventeen when they first met. Amos ventured over to her family farm to see if he could pick up some work. His family was poor, his clothes in tatters and he was barefoot. He must have looked a sight.

Even at her tender age, Katherine had the most beautiful brown eyes. And she was incredibly shy. Her dark hair was in plaits and tied with big yarn ribbons. She had been wearing a gingham dress and an oversized apron, probably her mother's. He thought she was the prettiest little thing he had ever seen.

Katherine—Katty, as her mother called her—looked the part of a milk maid, but had no idea what she was doing. Their old cow was expressing her displeasure at her awkward attempts at milking her which did nothing to dim her persistence.

Amos' father, Karl, was a drinker and stayed away from home most of the time. Amos thought that was just fine. When his father was home, his parents argued constantly. And when he finished with her, he would start in on the boys, calling them lazy and shiftless. He had good sons who worked from sunup to sundown trying to help their mother keep food on the table and a fire in the stove

Katty's father had hired him on the spot and came to treat him like a son. Amos worked hard for him to show his appreciation. He proved to be a trustworthy hand. He and Katherine became fast friends, almost like brother and sister, but he couldn't help stealing glances at her. He always thought she was too good for him. She didn't act that way and her family never treated him that way either.

One time her father came upon Amos' dad beating him while in a drunken rage. He thought his son had been withholding money from him. A violent fight ensued between the two men because his father kept trying to get at Amos.

His father left that night and never returned. His mother was heartbroken at first, hating to see her marriage fail, but somehow they managed. She took in sewing and laundry to help feed her young sons. That was Momma, always putting her family first. They all loved her dearly and did all they could to help her in the fields, cutting wood, hunting, fishing, doing anything they could to help ease her load.

When Amos was twenty, he had apprenticed with a man in the next village to learn tannery. He was thrilled at the chance encounter and the new opportunity. At first, he would come home late in the evening and have to leave out early the next morning. The man he was working with wanted him to stay in the village. He gave him a small attic room and his meals. Amos was earning a pittance which he sent to his mother. But, he was learning a good trade and was grateful this man had decided to take him under his wing.

His wife was kindly, almost like a mother to him. They had no children and she doted on him. She suspected that the young man had never had an easy life. Her husband would complain that she would make him soft. Amos felt loved and appreciated while living with them. He stayed with them for four short years, returning home at Christmas, in the early spring to help with the garden, and in the late summer to help his family put up the crops for winter. His brothers were big strong boys and took great care of his mother. She missed him but was relieved to see him making something of his life.

Amos rarely had a chance to go by his old friend Katherine's place because of his strict work schedule. He helped his mother set up her little roadside stand to sell her garden vegetables. And one day, helping her, he had looked up and spotted the most beautiful woman he had ever seen. She was tall with a willowy figure and the prettiest brown eyes which were somehow hauntingly familiar.

Katty couldn't believe her eyes when she saw the handsome, tanned and muscular young man helping her neighbor. She didn't recognize him at first. As she approached their eyes met, and a slow smile curved her lips.

She was still shy, but so beautiful. Amos couldn't take his eyes off her face. She seemed a little embarrassed but her eyes followed him. He had to be doing well with his new line of work. He was certainly dressing nicer than she had remembered.

Shortly after they met again, a proper courtship ensued from that day at the little vegetable stand. He called on her for nearly three years before her father pulled him aside one day. "Son," he'd said, "let's you and me take a little walk."

Amos felt his brow break out into sweat and his heart pound in his chest. He didn't know what to expect and feared that he had somehow upset this man who meant the world to him.

Her father strolled along in silence for awhile which did nothing to calm Amos's case of the nerves. Finally, he stopped and they leaned on the rail fence that marked the border of their pasture.

"Amos," he said, "let me ask you, what exactly are your intentions towards my daughter?"

Amos stammered, "Sir, I love her and I believe she loves me. I just don't feel like I'm worthy to ask for her hand. I don't have much to offer. I will stop coming around if you think its best."

Her father had laughed. "Son, if you do that, I'm sure neither my wife, nor my daughter, will ever speak to me again. They will be convinced that I somehow managed to run you off and spoiled her only chance for happiness. Oh no, you aren't putting that off on me!"

"Sir, May I marry your daughter if she will have me?" Amos could barely get the words out, he was so nervous. He loved this man and his whole family. He had been more like a father to him than his own.

"Amos, you'd be a welcome member of my family. It seems like you are already family, we've known you so long."

That night, alone on a walk with Katherine, he asked her to marry him. She started crying. He put his hat in his hand and hung his head. He was sure he just made a mess of things.

Katherine had reached out and touched his cheek and said, "Yes Amos. Of course I will."

They married a few months after that.

There was scarcely a dry eye in the living room when Amos finished his tale. Rachel handed the baby to Fletcher's mother. She crossed the room and hugged her father tightly. "I love you, Daddy. These are hard times, but we will both get through this."

Later, when Amos was finally alone at the house with his deceased bride and his memories, he reflected on days gone by. Katherine was an only child and her parents pestered them unmercifully about giving them a grandchild once they were married.

"We're not getting any younger, you know," her mother said.

After nearly ten years, her parents had been about to give up and suspected the two young people could not conceive a child. They were overjoyed to finally hear that Katherine was expecting. She became ill and they assumed it was just the pregnancy causing her malady. And at long last, she gave birth to a healthy baby girl.

Katherine's health seemed to continue to decline and Amos feared he might have to raise the child alone. She never seemed to regain her strength.

Katherine loved her husband and child. She often fretted about being such a burden to them, but neither one of them would hear of it. He still thought she was the most beautiful woman he had ever seen. Now, he could see Katherine's beauty in their daughter. He was forever grateful that the good Lord saw fit to have Rachel look like her mother instead of him.

Now, Amos went into their bedroom. The room was spotless and the bed was neatly made up. He took a blanket from the small wardrobe, climbed upon the bed and fell fast asleep on top of the bedcovers.

When he awoke, he realized that today was the day he would have to bury the love of his life. It was a gray day. Amos quickly dressed and prepared himself mentally as much as possible for this day's demands. He went to his wife's side and told her goodbye one last time. The men from the church showed up shortly afterward. After a couple of them took Amos for a walk down the lane with, the other fellows placed Katherine in the simple wooden coffin, loaded it gently onto the wagon and headed towards the cemetery.

Rachel and Fletcher came by to accompany Amos to the unpretentious service. A gentle rain was falling, but it was an unseasonably warm day. Her father's shoulders shook with the heartbreak of his loss. His life seemed so empty already without her. The service was simple and brief, but beautifully done. As they left the cemetery, the clouds broke and the sun shone brightly as they started home.

Suddenly, Amos saw the brightest double rainbow as they rode along. He thought *You and me, Katherine. That rainbow is beautiful but it couldn't hold a candle to what you and I had. I'll see you again someday, my precious little milk maid.*

After the funeral, he went with Rachel to her and Fletcher's home. He held Rachel's newborn baby and watched while her older son played quietly at his Papa's feet.

Oh Katherine, he thought. *How I wish you and I could have more time together to watch these two grow up.*

He saw his daughter's tear-streaked face and witnessed the liquid love pouring out for her mother. Rachel always was a devoted daughter and her mother had loved her dearly. Rachel was always such a blessing to them both, especially during this difficult time. Amos didn't know how he would have managed without her loving presence urging him on.

Folks always assumed that Katherine's illness was a millstone to him and his daughter, but they couldn't have been more wrong. What hurt him more than words could express was that he had not been by her side when she died. More than likely, she had passed while he was off getting the doctor. It was a guilt he would carry with him to his grave. If only he had known that day was going to be her last day on Earth. He had no way of knowing if she had suffered unnecessarily or if he could have done something, if not to save her, then at least, to comfort her.

He could have at least kissed her warm lips, held her in his arms and avowed his love for her one last time. He had to console himself with the knowledge of that peaceful expression on her lovely face. At last her torment was done. Folks always said those words, but it didn't make his life without her any easier.

CHAPTER 6

Fletcher

The mind of man plans his way, but the LORD directs his steps.

Proverbs 16:9

The next two years in Germany were very busy ones for Fletcher and his family. He, along with his father and his brother, worked hard at the farm. They shared in the labor and the fruits of it. They managed to grow enough for their personal use and to keep a little vegetable stand stocked. A couple of grocers in town bought from his father, too. The men hunted and fished on the weekends when they could.

Fletcher's children were growing and kept Rachel busy chasing after them. Watching Rachel playing with them always caught at Fletcher's heart. She was such a natural mother. She seemed like just a child herself. Childbirth and the chores of their simple farm life had done nothing to dim her spirit.

In the spring of 1919, he planted that year's garden. The weather and the soil cooperated and the harvest was better than it had been in years. They stored the root vegetables in the cellar and canned what they could. He and his father salted away enough meat to last their family through the coming year. Even longer, if it came to that.

Fletcher worked on all the small odd jobs at their home that he had put off for one reason or another. He knew all this work was necessary, but really all he wanted to do was hold his wife and children. He wanted to stare into their eyes and felt like he had so much he wanted to tell them.

Rachel often teased him about having his head in the clouds. But lately he'd had reason. He felt each new day brought them even less freedom and greater government involvement in the affairs of his homeland.

Fletcher didn't think of himself as a political activist or rebel, but he did feel that his core values were under attack. Why couldn't things just stay the same? There was an odd, yet precious peace in being largely ignored and allowed to live out your life as your forefathers had.

The men down at the square talked of even more government control. It shocked him to think that the German government could take ownership of his own property. As if that was not enough, there was talk of government censorship of religion. He and Rachel both were raised in God-fearing homes. He could not imagine not being able to attend meetings with fellow believers or even being told what their beliefs should be. Because Bibles were few and far between in his little hamlet, he had listened closely in church and memorized verses that seemed to speak to his heart. Why, didn't the Holy Bible say, *Gather the people together, men and women, and children, and thy stranger that is within thy gates, that they may hear, and that they may learn, and fear the LORD your God, and observe to do all the words of this law?*

Fletcher heard talk of the opportunities in America. He had friends there, and they'd written and encouraged him to join them. They had talked about the upcoming opening of the Big Vein coal mine in the little village of McCoy in Montgomery County, Virginia. Superior Anthracite Coal Company, headquartered in Baltimore, had begun hiring and training their initial workers. They were looking for other able bodied and hardworking men. That certainly described Fletcher. He had a strong constitution and didn't mind hard work.

The fellows Fletcher knew were eking out a living in tents and army-like camp arrangements. They pooled their supplies, and shared in the expense of necessities and chores of their little community. They typically walked the handful of miles into town once a week to replenish their supplies. Occasionally, they caught a ride with a local farmer on the back of his wagon. It was not uncommon for them to each squirrel away more than half of their earnings. They were willing to make sacrifices to expedite the length of time until their families could join them. Many of the men wrote of being homesick, but hard work and exhaustion proved to be just the elixir for what ailed them.

Fletcher, strangely, was not having any second thoughts about leaving his homeland. His home was wherever his family was. Eventually he and Rachel settled on travelling to the little town of Blacksburg, Virginia. Their friends mentioned the beautiful blue Appalachian mountains and the vast meadows. Game, he had heard, was plentiful. Fletcher's father had given him a great new rifle to take with him to the new country.

Rachel encouraged him to pursue his dreams and supported his decision to leave for America wholeheartedly. Or so it seemed. His heart ached at the thought of leaving her and the boys behind. Their children were so young. He feared they would forget about him. He was going to miss so many firsts with them. Fletcher knew too that they could be a handful and worried about Rachel managing them by herself. But he would see them soon.

His parents assured him that they would keep an eye on Rachel and the boys. His mother just had two sons and thought of her daughters-in-law as her own daughters. She felt especially close to Rachel since she had picked her for her younger son. His brother and sister-in-law lived just down the way and had promised to help out with his little brood. It sounded like it was all worked out.

Fletcher tried to convince his mother and father to come with them to America but their hearts were set on staying right where they were. This was the only home they knew. His mother cried when she heard that her son and his family would be leaving, but his father was supportive. "You are a man now with a family," he told Fletcher. "You have to make the decisions that you think are best for them. Your mother would like to keep you all neatly tucked beneath her wing for the rest of her life. That's just the God-given instinct that women are given. There comes a time when every fellow has to look about him, test the direction of the wind and make tough choices."

It was a moment before Fletcher spoke. "I can understand why mother would be concerned. But you're right. I have to do this."

He didn't express it, but his father's heart swelled with pride at his son's ambition. He was proud of his youngest son. Yes, this boy had a good head on his shoulders. Whatever decision he and Rachel made, he and his wife would support it.

CHAPTER 7

To the Shore

In all your ways acknowledge Him, And He shall direct your paths.

Proverbs 3:6

He and Rachel slept little the night before he left. They talked the morning through about their hopes, dreams and fears. He held her close and felt her tremble. He finally drifted off to sleep just before sunrise and woke up an hour later. It was going to be a long day.

They all decided that his Papa would take him as far as the next village. There he hoped to find a series of rides to the shore. He would board the merchant ship that was docked for the next week in the bay at the booming seaport city. It would take him across the Atlantic to start their new life. Fletcher arranged that he would work aboard the ship as a hand to help offset the expense of the voyage. He had no seafaring experience but he could offer a strong back and a good mind. He was willing to learn whatever new skills he needed to from the rest of the crew. They wouldn't have to be concerned about him upholding his part of the bargain.

Rachel wanted to ride with them to the village, but he thought she looked a little peaked. Her stomach had been bothering her, especially early in the morning. She told him it was probably just nerves over him leaving. He was so caught up in his own plans for the crossover that it never occurred to him that there might be more to it.

Fletcher's family walked with him down the lane as he left. Rachel put on a brave front, but was smiling just a little too much. Her eyes were bright and he knew her well enough to know she was holding back tears. She wouldn't want to upset him or the boys. The children skipped ahead. He and Rachel held hands as they continued down the path. They had so many sweet memories together in their little house and on this patch of land, and it hurt deep in his heart to leave them behind.

When they reached the end of the road, Fletcher took her face in his hands and stared into her eyes. He kissed her full lips and she held her breath. He pulled her tightly into his arms. Her head rested snugly and perfectly on his broad shoulder. He leaned his head over hers feeling the warm sunshine on her wavy locks. She smelled so fresh and wholesome.

He tilted her chin up towards his face. Her eyes still brimmed with tears. She quickly wiped them away and sniffled slightly.

"I love you," he said. "Leaving you and the boys is the hardest thing I've ever had to do."

"We will be all right," Rachel said. "It's not like you are leaving us alone. We are surrounded by family. But we'll worry about you. You're the one crossing the ocean."

Joseph and Arwood, distracted by a bird hopping along on the fence, were giggling and running ahead. Rachel called them over. She wasn't sure that they understood that their Daddy wouldn't be coming home at the end of the day. He'd never spent time away from them.

Arwood toddled over and hugged his father. He planted a big sloppy kiss on his father's cheek. Fletcher hugged him tight. Joseph dawdled over. Fletcher picked him up and whirled him around until giggles tumbled out.

He took both of them in his arms. "I love you," he said. "Remember what we talked about. Help your mother." He smiled. "Joseph, you'll be the man of the house while I'm gone. Of course that doesn't mean that you don't have to listen to your mother. Even I had to do that."

Rachel smiled at him as he looked at her over the heads of his children. "I love you," he whispered.

They heard the familiar clopping sound of their Papa coming down the lane. The little boys hurried down the lane to see their grandfather. John stepped down and gave them both big hugs. He watched his youngest son give his wife one last kiss. He noticed Rachel's weak smile. He'd get Hilda to come by and check on them later.

Fletcher put his one bag up in the wagon and climbed up front with his Papa. He looked back and waved to his family. They all stood and watched him leave until he was out of sight. It was a momentous day and, as only men can do, they traveled along mostly in silence, each man caught up in his own thoughts.

His Papa dropped him off and gave him a bag of sandwiches and cookies his mother had made. John didn't tell his son about the challenge it had been keeping her at the house. He didn't want to send his son off with the memory of his teary-eyed Mama making a fool of herself. To her, he would always be her baby. She just couldn't understand his drive to leave his home and family. Meaning her, of course.

"Son," he said, "you'll let us know if you need anything, won't you? You know we don't have much, but whatever we do have, it's yours."

"I know, Papa. You and Mama have given me everything I need. You've raised me the best you could, taught me the difference between right and wrong, helped me get an education, and taught me the things I needed to know to grow my own crops, work on my house, and take care of our animals. It's more than enough."

"It hasn't been much," his father said. "I just don't know what life will be like for you in that strange place."

They said their farewells at the crossroads. Fletcher stood watching his father's wagon as the horse sauntered down the lane. He wondered if he would ever see his Mama and Papa again. That was something that none of them had voiced, but it must have been at the back of their minds all this time. He noticed how lined his Papa's face was becoming and how he didn't seem as agile as he used to. His Papa seemed so calm, but his Mama was always so het up about things, good or bad, she was just a nervous person. They were a good match. She could boost him up and he could hold her back. Fletcher chuckled to himself thinking about that. That was what worked for their relationship.

There were no wagons on the road yet, so Fletcher picked up his little sack and began to hike along the road. He was lost in his thoughts as he ambled along. The morning was heating up and his brow was beginning to sweat from the exertion. He had been walking for a little over an hour. The slow clop of horse hooves caught him by surprise.

"Morning, young man. You are out and about awfully early today aren't you? Where are you headed?" a wizened farmer asked him.

His rickety old wagon was loaded with hay that he was delivering to the next town for a gentleman there.

"Good morning," Fletcher said. "I'm traveling to the seaside to go to work on a ship."

The old farmer looked him up and down. "Well, pardon me for saying so, but you look more like a farmer than a sailor to me."

Fletcher laughed. It helped. He didn't realize how tightly wound he had been this morning.

"You've got that right. If that farm you're headed to is in my direction, I'd be obliged to catch a ride. I can give you a hand unloading the hay."

He offered Fletcher some water from his jug. "I could use the company. Hop on up here. Take the reins if you'd like and I'll rest up. We've got another hour or so to go."

Fletcher eagerly accepted. The water was cool, as if it had just been drawn from a deep well. The old farmer turned over the reins to Fletcher. He kept up a lively chatter for a little while, and then grew strangely quiet. When Fletcher glanced over, he had to smile. The poor fellow was fast asleep. No telling how early he had gotten up that morning to load that wagon. Fletcher could only hope someone had helped the man with the chore.

After they finished with the hay the farmer's wife invited them to stay and have a bite with them. She served thinly sliced bologna sandwiches with tomato slices, a little spiced mustard and a large dill pickle wedge. Afterwards, Fletcher rode with the old farmer back out to the main road where they parted company.

The old gent thought he might have just met an angel. He certainly appreciated the help with the hay and the drive. The company had been a treat too. He lived alone and took whatever work he could find to get along.

Over the next four days, Fletcher managed to catch several rides and walked when he couldn't. He slept in barns, on front porches, in sheds and once under a tree, using his jacket for a pillow.

At long last, he could tell he had almost reached the shore; he could smell the salty air and hear the birds of the sea long before he could actually see the water. He was weary from his travels. But still, he didn't want to waste any of his precious too few coins getting a room at an inn. He desperately needed a shave and a bath. He worked up a sweat unloading that hay. Fletcher spotted a barber shop and made his way over. The place was practically empty. He asked the barber for a recommendation of a place to get a bath and change his clothes.

The man looked him over and said, "I live back behind here. For a couple of coins, you can use my place and my missus will probably throw in a little supper."

Fletcher thanked him for his hospitality.

CHAPTER 8

Ship Passage

He who heeds the word wisely will find good, And whoever trusts in the LORD, *happy is he.*

Proverbs 16:20

After supper he headed down to the docks to look for his ship. He hoped the captain would be on board so he could negotiate his passage. As it turned out, he was in luck, the captain was just returning from having his own supper. The two men shook hands. Captain Nelson explained what work he had for him and assigned him a bunk.

That bed with the blanket-thin mattress looked fine to Fletcher. His job sounded simple enough: he was to assist the ship's cook. Blessed as he was by the women in his life, Fletcher didn't know a thing about kitchen duties.

The captain laughed heartily at the shocked expression on the young man's face. "Don't worry. You'll be lugging sacks of potatoes and onions, chopping vegetables, making bread and the likes before you reach that far shore. You can probably expect to become pretty handy at washing dishes too."

His pipe left a thin blue flume behind his head as he made his way out of the galley. "Aye, your wife will be right proud of your new skills when she sees you next."

This was not exactly the seafaring work Fletcher had fantasized about. In fact, he thought it was downright embarrassing. But he swallowed his pride. He would be able to save his money as well as be able to pocket a little extra for his efforts.

Most of the other working men aboard ship had not returned from shore leave. The captain didn't expect to see them until the day before the boat launched. Most of them made their homes in the busy seaport. The crew welcomed a chance to be home with their families for a few weeks before it became time to hit the water again.

Fletcher used the downtime to explore the layout of the ship. Just the size of it was hard to grasp, and it was hard for him to imagine how it could float and not just sink. He thought of skimming rocks across the water as a child and how they eventually sank. Best not to dwell on that. This ship had made many a trip back and forth across the ocean.

The passage to the States was much tougher than the trip back home for the crew. This was a big, sturdy merchant ship. It got loaded at various ports along the way and came back brimming with supplies local business owners in Germany needed to meet the needs of the town folk. They would bring everything from hardware, nails, and exotic plants, to fine bolts of fabric and perfume.

Everyone anxiously awaited the arrival of the vessel on its home shore. Sure, there was the labor of loading and unloading the ship, but that was quickly dispensed with. Afterwards. the men had their time to themselves, provided that no storms blew up that demanded their time and skill.

The trip to the States filled the ship with people emigrating to some strange new place. Most of those passengers had never been on a ship in their life. So, along with them came all their problems, complaints, needs, heartaches, sea sickness, screaming children, families arguing. The men would much rather guard some silent box of hammers or thread. But, it was their livelihood and it was expensive to take the big tub across the ocean without some sort of commerce to offset the cost. And steady work was hard to come by.

The ship Fletcher was on could carry some ten thousand pounds of cargo and three hundred passengers. When sailing with just passengers, however, it could hold around two thousand, making it resemble a village floating on the sea. Most emigrating families traveled together. Some were paupers, the government had paid to leave; some were poor, like Fletcher. The well-heeled were much smaller in number. The better educated German emigrants tended to fall between the poor and the well-heeled, depending on how long they had been surviving on their bankroll.

For the most part, the captain had the same crew voyage after voyage. He could rest assured that they would conduct themselves properly regardless of the responsibility dealt them. Occasionally, he would need to hire on a fellow or two, usually by reference from past captains. Now and then he ended up with some scallywags who did nothing but stir up trouble among the rank and file. He knew how to deal with that sort; he simply banned them from the ship at the next port, leaving them to fend for themselves with a small payment for their services.

He didn't have a problem with the men working for him having a drink or two, or playing a little card game to relax; he knew that usually involved some gambling, too. This was a ship not a church, after all. It wasn't his responsibility to be their conscience. What was it to him if they gambled away their earnings?

One thing he would not tolerate, however, was someone with a serious drinking problem. That usually meant they had a working and disciplinary problem to go along with it. He had traveled these seas for too many years to put up with such behavior. They certainly never asked him for a referral for the next captain because it wouldn't take them very far. They gave him a wide berth when they saw him, because he was well respected by the other ship's captains who would listen to his summary of their performance under his leadership.

Fletcher slept well in the hard little bunk on the shifting sea. It was like being gently rocked to sleep. He sprang out of bed that next morning and climbed out of the belly of the ship. He had slept much later than was usual for him.

It was a beautiful morning. Hard to believe he left home five days ago. Fletcher thought he would spend the morning exploring the bustling seaport of Hamburg. It definitely appeared that he had arrived in the land of have and have-nots. He noticed folks dressed in much finery dining at various outside venues at Lake Alster. Fletcher had never seen so many people in one place and wondered if this was how America was going to be.

He grabbed a croissant and some rather strong coffee and sat down at a modest little pub's outside table to enjoy his breakfast. A man sitting nearby greeted him. Fletcher asked him if he knew much about the coastal city.

The fellow turned out to be a well educated gentleman and somewhat of a local historian. He welcomed the opportunity to talk about the place he loved and had lived all his life. He attempted to give Fletcher the lay of the land, or in this case, the waterways.

He gestured broadly with his arms, like a stage performer. "The North Sea is to the west of Hamburg and to the northeast lays the Baltic Sea. Hamburg is a major transport hub, almost everything coming into or leaving Germany filters through this little sea of humanity."

He leaned forward, happy to speak to his knowledge. "Hamburg is located on the River Elbeat which joins two other rivers, the Alster and Bille. The River Alster was once dammed up to form lakes in and around the city. Those lakes make it possible for vessels to move freely about to deliver their cargo without so much unpacking and repacking. It is all about business, you see."

Fletcher nodded and agreed, thinking of his time selling extra vegetables from his farm.

The man went on. "One of my favorite things to do is come and sit in this very spot and watch the comings and goings of the ships, the sailors, Germany's outpouring of emigrating population and of course, the locals. If only I was a great writer, so I could give life to my speculations about the people and their lives that pass through this great city. I never intend to be eavesdropping in on conversations but really it can't be helped, not here." He grinned conspiratorially. "I guess you could say my life's work is to study human nature. I like to think about the who, what, how and why we all do what we do. And sitting here each morning, I have a wealth of people to observe."

The man took a sip of his drink. "Hamburg is divided into seven boroughs, each of them with their own unique personalities, shall we say. There are streams, rivers and canals and must be thousands of bridges that cross them. And if a bridge doesn't cross the waterway, then have no fear, because there are many ferries available. We certainly earn the name of a water town, don't we?"

Fletcher was amazed at the man's knowledge and storytelling skills. Fletcher had only the most rudimentary education, but listening to this gentleman made him realize how little he knew about his own country. In a different time and place, he could have sought adventure and opportunity in his own backyard, he thought. The man's voice interrupted his musings.

"Young man, if you get time, try to see the St Nicholas church. It is rumored to be one of the world's tallest buildings. Of course, not having done any traveling myself, I can't vouch for the accuracy of that claim. Then, there is the Town Hall with all its fancy decoration. It is covered with images of emperors of the Holy Roman Empire. That's quite a sight to behold. Of course, we learn about an area by many experiences, but you must sample Bimen, Bohnen und Speck. It is a delicious dish which contains green beans, pears and bacon. I couldn't tell you how to make it, just that it is delicious. It sounds a little suspicious doesn't it? Then there is the Aalsuppe. Many call this dish eel soup. The funny thing is, it doesn't usually contain anything so exotic, just a little of all the chef's scraps of food is what it looks like to me, but somehow it manages to turn out well. Must have something to do with the spices or how they prepare it."

Fletcher's stomach growled, interrupting the man's soliloquy. They both laughed. Fletcher apologized and talked with the man for a bit about his own aspirations for a new life in America. The gentleman leaned in, listening intently, excited to bear witness to the young man's heart for his family and dreams of a better life for them. This was a rare experience for the older man to have someone talk so freely. He tried unsuccessfully on many occasions to coax folks into telling him their stories, but found them reluctant to talk. Many may have thought he had something to do with the government and that talking with him would come to no good.

The men shook hands and Fletcher went on his way. He walked down the boardwalk, admired the many ships docked there and the amazing architecture of the ancient buildings the man had mentioned. The weather was perfect. The day was winding down as he headed back towards his ship to meet the cook and begin the work of a cook's helper.

He managed to stop by a little seaside restaurant and sample the Aalsuppe the fellow had referred to. He chuckled as he wolfed it down. He'd been expecting some sort of delicacy and this tasted like the same old soup his Mama and wife had been feeding him for years!

Fletcher learned his new responsibilities on the ship quickly and enjoyed working with the old cook, Claude. Claude could be a little salty in his discourse when challenged or questioned by the sailors about his choice ingredients in the simple fare he served up. Fletcher just assumed that all cooks must be temperamental. He learned long ago to just eat what was put in front of him, go heavy on the praise and lightly on any criticism.

His sea trip was uneventful, no big storms and good workmen alongside him. In the little over two months it took for the commute, everything went smoothly. The captain had given the word that they would make landfall in a matter of days.

CHAPTER 9

Ellis Island

For surely there is a hereafter, And your hope will not be cut off.

Proverbs 23:18

Fletcher packed his bag to disembark from the merchant ship when it approached the New York port in late November, 1919. He collected his wages and tied his money up in a handkerchief and placed it in the one bag he had brought onboard. He located the captain to tell him goodbye.

"Thank you for allowing me to come over on your ship," Fletcher said. "I hope I haven't disappointed you."

"Son, if this mining job you are thinking about doesn't work out; you come back and look me up. I wish I had other men who would work half as hard as you." The captain extended his hand.

Fletcher shook it. "I'm not sure I will be anymore help to my wife and mother in the kitchen than I have been, but at least now, I will appreciate them more. This woman's work is harder than it looks."

The old captain just grinned and nodded at the young man. "Good luck, son. I hope you find all you're looking for. I will keep an eye on your family for you when they are ready to join you. Tell them to please introduce themselves to me."

Fletcher joined the throng of people leaving the big steamship and entering the ferry which would take them to Ellis Island. The ships were too large to come any closer. He'd gotten a good night's rest and was eager to set foot on American soil. He wondered if he would ever be able to sleep again without the gentle lull of the ocean rocking him.

He and the other emigrants all crammed tightly onto the ferry. It looked like a sea of people were awaiting their turn. Fletcher was traveling light, but he observed men, women and children all carrying various size bundles that represented all their life possessions. To him, they looked like they were headed to a fair. Everyone was dressed in their very best, right down to their hats, bonnets and scarves. Many of the men were wearing suits they probably reserved for church or special occasions. Fletcher looked the part of a farmer. His clothes were simple, but clean and had no holes that he was aware of.

On the ferry, he managed to get a standing spot by the railing. He watched the sun jubilantly bouncing off the waves. As he looked around him, he observed the faces of the people around him. He saw happy smiles, some were singing and kids were jumping up and down in excitement. Some folks were crying. Seeing so many children made Fletcher lonesome for his two young sons.

Fletcher looked back towards the water. It was a cold winter's day, but the sky was sunny and the air crisp. He pulled his jacket close to block the wind. He bowed his head and thanked God for his safe passage. He asked Him to watch over his family and to bring them over safely when they were able to come.

It seemed like no time at all before the ferry reached the island. Fletcher saw for the first time what he considered the true symbol of America, the Statue of Liberty. She stood tall and proud and had a beautiful green patina. He couldn't be sure but the flame, at the end of the arm which was raised high in the air, appeared to be stained glass. The sunlight was shining brightly through the flame giving off a host of beautiful colors.

This is why they were all coming: for life, liberty and the pursuit of happiness. Sounded almost like marriage vows…except for that liberty part, Fletcher thought with a grin. She was certainly a grand lady and as Fletcher looked about him, it seemed no one could take their eyes off of her. Regardless of their wealth, status, or lack thereof, each in his or her own way was taking a big chance. They had all come to this new country, not knowing what to expect, but were each so full of hope and expectation.

As they stepped off the ferry, Fletcher noticed that other ferries were also delivering passengers as well. It was very noisy and confusing at the busy port. So many different languages, mothers screaming for their children to stick with them, not to wander off, men shouting to each other. Everyone seemed to be in an enormous hurry. They were like so many head of cattle, being herded to a big building that Fletcher thought looked like a castle of some sort.

There must have been hundreds of Americans working with the immigrants in one way or another. Many of the people were in uniforms, like police. When he got inside, he found a bathroom. It was clean enough given how many people were streaming through this place. The plumbing interested him. There was a larger sink for washing up and a smaller sink for spitting. Fletcher had never taken up the tobacco or snuff habit. It did feel good to wash his hands and splash some warm water on his face.

Fletcher thought the architecture was beautiful in the impressive structure the workers called the Ferry building, Fletcher was directed to get in line for his health screening. The place was teeming with doctors and nurses. Every one of them was working as hard as they could. Their job was to ensure that the people coming through didn't have infectious diseases. Some were detained and sent up to the second floor which was an enormous hospital ward. The medical screening took better than three hours because there were so many people ahead of him.

The folks in line both before and behind him, complained unceasingly about the wait. The children cried whether because they were bored, hungry, sleepy or sick. Mothers screeched at them, all in all it was loud and more than a little overwhelming. There were benches that folks could sit on. With the number of women and children there, Fletcher did not sit. He hated the thought of Rachel having to endure all this by herself with their two boys.

When Fletcher was finally at the front of the line, his health screening went smoothly and he was given a piece of paper which had been stamped "Approved." He was then directed to the next leg of his processing to the legal section in the big Registry room. This was another long corridor of metal railings and it seemed like just as many people as before waiting ahead of him.

He looked ahead and saw walls of filing cabinets. He saw harried personnel checking off information in a series of large ledgers. Serious looking clerks looked so weary as they processed the new immigrants, one by one. He asked one of the workers what this was all about.

The kindly older gentleman explained that the United States had immigration laws which prohibited some people from entering this country. If they were convicted criminals, anarchists, or even sometimes paupers, they could be deported and refused admittance.

Fletcher wondered if he would have to produce his little wad of money to prove he was not exactly a pauper, even if he was maybe close.

The inspectors here sat at tall desks and had the ships' manifesto describing each passenger. When he finally reached the front of this line, the first question they asked him was his name and the name of the ship he had arrived on. They located his information quickly. It was in order and a clerk handed him his pass.

At last, Fletcher was on his way down the long flight of stairs that led him out of the ferry building. He had purchased his ticket and was on his way. While waiting in the long lines, he had learned of a railroad system in New Jersey. There was a ferry that would take him that direction, though he was afraid it would cost too much. The ferry he boarded would take him to lower Manhattan in New York City. From there, he would work his way to Pittsburgh, Pennsylvania to board a train that would eventually deliver him to Roanoke, Virginia. *What a lovely sounding name for a state,* he thought. Like a beautiful lady.

As he stepped off the ferry, Fletcher realized he had not eaten all day. A nurse had given him some water earlier. Someone had come around with food at one time while he was at the ferry building, but it didn't seem like enough to feed all those hungry people, especially women and children. Fletcher had declined their offer of a sandwich. His stomach was reminding him that he had a responsibility to himself as well as others.

He found a little restaurant and went inside. The Frenchman who worked there sold him a croissant filled with ham and cheese, lettuce and tomato. At that moment, Fletcher thought it was probably the best thing he had eaten in his life. He had a hot cup of coffee and splurged on a small pastry.

It was around six that evening when Fletcher walked outside the restaurant. He stretched his long, lean body. It seemed like a great deal of time had passed since he had gotten off the ship. At home, he had always felt special, being the youngest son, loved by his family and respected by the folks in the hamlet because of his good work ethic and Christian values. Going through the Ellis Island screening process made him realize that in this big city, there were thousands just like him. That revelation was very humbling.

Fletcher entered the street and began to explore about to see how best he could get to Pennsylvania. He noticed some men loading boxes on a wagon. He walked over to see if he could lend a hand. They eyed him suspiciously. Work was hard to find in this part of the city. They did not welcome competition especially not from someone young and healthy.

Fletcher quickly explained that he was just looking for a ride that would move him farther down the line. He told the two fellows he didn't expect any monetary payment. He was interested in a ride, if they were going in the right direction.

One of the men looked at the other and said, "What do you think, Hank?"

"I don't see any harm in it. We're going about three hours due west. We can take you that far. You're not some kind of crook are you?"

Fletcher assured them he was not a criminal of any sort, and rolled up his sleeves. *"Would a crook answer that question honestly?, wondered Fletcher"*

Working together, the three men made short order of the job. Fletcher climbed on the back of the loaded wagon and the men set off. At the other end of the journey, he once again helped the men unload their cargo and thanked for them for the ride. The men smiled, thinking that they had definitely come out on the better end of their bargain. They wished him well and headed back towards the city.

Fletcher walked a ways and found an old abandoned house to spend the night. He built a fire in the fireplace with some old wood scraps he found out behind the house. He hoped the place didn't burn down in the night.

He awoke before daybreak and decided to get on his way. As luck would have it, a wagon came up behind him. The two young brothers asked Fletcher if he'd like a ride into town. They were carrying eggs and milk to sell to the grocery stores and restaurants in the next couple of small towns. They were going his direction and once again Fletcher felt blessed. It seemed many times, things and people were going his way in this new country.

The boys shared some of the still warm biscuits their mother had made and packed for them that morning. They were smeared with homemade butter and the most delicious sweet grape jam.

"We can never eat all the food she packs for us," the younger boy lied.

"Well, it looks like you two are a couple of growing boys, Fletcher said. "You'll need it. I did."

As he journeyed along, Fletcher met several other nice families who gave him a place to stay and fed him a good meal. They all seemed to have a place in their heart for the sad looking young man with the friendly smile and funny accent. Yes, the good Lord was looking out for him in the form of all these angels He put in his path.

CHAPTER 10

Almost There!

Uphold my steps in Your paths, That my footsteps may not slip.

NKJR Psalm 17:5

The trip from the state of Pennsylvania fascinated Fletcher. This was his first train ride and he was impressed with the gigantic, powerful mechanical snake sliding down the two narrow tracks that seemed to go on forever. He watched the beautiful countryside rolling by as the engine slowly made its way into Roanoke Virginia. There were a number of people on the train, many of them immigrants such as him. He didn't meet anyone on the train who was traveling to Blacksburg.

Fletcher thought the train fare was a bit steep and he hated dipping into his meager funds. He reasoned that he might end up spending more money trying to hoof it by the time he bought meals. He had never ridden on a train before. It would be something to tell his sons about someday.

Fletcher was traveling light, with just the clothes on his back, his coat, black woolen scarf, hat and gloves Rachel had knitted him, his rifle and shells, a pocket knife, a small frying pan, a fork, one change of clothes, a small loaf of bread, and a hunk of cheese a generous older lady had insisted he take with him. Thoughts of Rachel filled his mind and heart with love and a sense of wistfulness.

Stepping off the train at his destination, he bristled at the still, crisp air. It seemed to go right through his warm jacket. If he wasn't mistaken, there was the smell of snow in the air. His papa laughed at Fletcher when he had made that statement around the age of twelve or so, when his papa, his brother and he were out hunting in the woods on their land.

"Son, what exactly does snow smell like?" his papa had teased.

Fletcher remembered scrunching up his nose and breathing in sharply the cold air before answering. "Pepper," he said.

His brother and Papa had laughed at him. They hunted early in the morning through early afternoon. As they turned towards home, it started snowing big flakes at first, then more densely, quickly covering the ground.

On the walk home his father had favored him with a sidelong glance. "That's a mighty fine nose you have there, young man."

Fletcher felt vindicated. And now, in the early evening, here in Roanoke, Virginia, he could smell that familiar scent once again. It was funny how it worked. Sometimes he was just as surprised as everyone else when it snowed, but other times, he got that whiff and just knew they were in for it. Fletcher sought directions to Blacksburg at the train station from the attendant. He set out in a southwesterly direction.

The mountainous hike wearied him. He took a swig of water from his jar, reminding himself to fill it up at the creek he noticed over the hillside. That is, if it wasn't frozen over by morning. Just before dark, he managed to shoot a rabbit for his dinner. He skinned and gutted it with the pocket knife Amos had given him for his nineteenth birthday.

He found the mouth of a small cave and checked it for occupants, man and beast alike. You just couldn't tell who or what you might encounter being on the road. Finding it empty, he set about making a small cook fire. He used his fork as a makeshift skewer. As he was cooking the meat he thought he heard a coyote's howl. Fletcher added more wood to his little fire. He certainly didn't need that kind of company tonight.

Soon his stomach was full. With the cave walls blocking the wind, his little shelter for the night was about as snug as he could expect on a December evening so far from home. Rachel would be worried to death if she could see him now. He didn't think she needed to know just how difficult this leg of his journey was, but it might be another story to add to his tales for his boys when they got a little older. He remembered his papa telling him stories of how he had roughed it growing up. Well, now Fletcher had a tale or two of his own.

Rachel. Hopefully, she and the boys would arrive in the summer and he could pick them up in a borrowed wagon. He wanted to do everything he could to make sure their trip was a little more comfortable than his had been so far.

Looking up at the curved ceiling of the cave, he prayed, "Now, Lord, I'm not complaining, mind you. I thank you for the safety I've had and the saints who have helped me along the way. I will need all the help I can get to get me through without my family. My strength comes from You, my Heavenly Father. Amen."

He got as comfortable as possible in his little abode for the night and quickly fell asleep.

At dawn he collected his belongings and stepped outside to meet the robust morning. Fletcher went by the creek and, using a stick he found on the bank, broke through the ice and refilled his water supply. As he straightened up and stretched, he felt blessed to see the sunrise shining over these peculiar, but beautiful, blue-ridged mountains. He gave a short and satisfied prayer of thanks.

Despite the cold, Fletcher enjoyed the slight warmth of the sunshine on his back as he began his trek up the mountain. As he walked, he thought of his mama and papa. He hoped they were doing well this winter. He worried that his Papa might overdo things without him there to help out. Hopefully, Peter would keep a watchful eye on their father. His Papa seemed to be at that particular age where he had bigger ideas than his physical strength would permit him to complete. Somehow, his father didn't seem to recognize that fact and tried to work right alongside his sons until he was completely given out.

Fletcher heard about older men having heart attacks when they overexerted. It had happened to fathers and grandfathers of men he knew. He hoped to have his father around for many more years to come, even if he wasn't coming to America with him.

CHAPTER 11

A Special Place

For I know the thoughts that I think toward you, says the LORD,
thoughts of peace and not of evil, to give you a future and a hope.

Jeremiah 29:11

When Fletcher finally made it to Blacksburg, he was surprised to see so much development. There was a Norfolk and Western railroad line, a college of higher learning, a bank, hotels, general store, grocery store, doctors, lawyers, church, newspaper and even a theater. Its industry reminded him more of Hamburg than his own little village.

He felt a little blinded by the glare of the snow he walked through that blustery day. Approaching the general store and its steamed windows, Fletcher cupped his frozen hands up to the glass and looked inside. He was relieved to find it was indeed open for business. Fletcher felt warm air as soon as he opened the big solid wooden door. He went directly to the little pot belly coal stove over in the corner. He noticed wooden barrels strategically placed all around the stove and a couple of older gents sitting peacefully smoking their pipes. The soda cracker barrels doubled as seats. It felt good to get off his feet for a bit.

Fletcher unbuttoned his coat, removed his hat and gloves, loosened his scarf and absorbed the blessed warmth. His toes felt like ice in his boots, but, he thought he better keep his shoes on. The two men seated in the corner nodded and exchanged knowing looks with each other. They had seen many a stranger getting his first taste of Blacksburg right here in this very spot. The store was like a lighthouse to tired wayfarers.

Fletcher nodded to the two men but didn't speak at first. They didn't seem to mind. After a bit of thawing out, he finally spoke. "I think I've fallen in love with a coal stove," he said, and the men laughed. "It's been a long haul. Hopefully, my traveling days are over for awhile."

One of the men asked, "You're German, aren't you son? What's your name?"

"Yes sir, that's right, I'm German. My name is Fletcher Broce. I left Hamburg's seaport in September. I worked aboard the merchant steamship that brought me to New York City about mid- November. From there, I travelled mostly on foot to Pennsylvania to catch the train to Roanoke. Two days walk brought me here. Frozen, but here."

The men laughed again. One of the fellows got up and went over towards the counter. His friend and Fletcher sat comfortably exchanging pleasantries.

When the other man reappeared, he was carrying a steaming cup of coffee and a large slice of cake. Fletcher's mouth watered. He started mentally adding up his money to decide if he could afford to indulge his craving. While Fletcher was musing, the older man came over and sat the coffee and cake down in front of Fletcher.

"You look like you could use a little nourishment, young man. Welcome to Blacksburg."

"What do I owe you, sir?"

"Nothing. You just try to return the favor for another poor soul someday when you can. We see a great many new faces coming to our town these days. It's just a little gesture of friendship."

The outpouring of generosity amazed Fletcher. "I don't know what to say. Thank you, sir. I'm afraid I don't even know your name."

"I'm William Harvey. Most folks call me Bill. This here fellow is Roland Price. We call him Slim. You can probably take a good look at him and figure out how he got that nickname."

Fletcher smiled and said, "I can guarantee you it was not from eating cake like this."

Fletcher must have been at the store close to an hour. He didn't have a watch, so he hadn't ready kept track of the time. Bill and Slim talked about their farms, their gardens and their families, but mostly about their grandchildren.

Fletcher wondered if his mama and papa did the same thing: talk about his boys to anyone who would listen. They certainly were doting grandparents. He told Bill and Slim about Rachel and his boys. The old men could hear the wistfulness in the young man's voice.

"Now, son," Slim said. "Buck up. It won't be any time before your young lady and sons are here with you. Take it from me: sometimes, it can seem like a long time when you're waiting on something to happen, and then, it's here before you know it."

Bill agreed, "Yes, that's true. I know it's hard to be away from your family at Christmas. I'm guessing this is the longest you've ever been away from home."

Fetcher nodded agreeably and pushed his chair back. "Gentlemen, I have enjoyed your company. Thanks for making me feel welcome and thank you for that cake and coffee. I guess I better get a few things together and head out before I lose anymore of this day."

"Pleased to meet you," Bill said, and Slim echoed him.

Fletcher stood up, stretched and made his way to the long wooden counter where the storekeeper and his wife stood. He greeted them both.

"I'm Bert Tilley," the man said. "This is my wife, Eloise. We've lived in these parts all our lives. Where are you heading?"

"Actually, I'm not sure which direction to head next. I'm hoping you can help me with that."

"I guess you will be going to the German work camp, right?"

"Yes, there are men already there from my part of Germany. It will be good to see some familiar faces. I'm hoping to get on at the mines. I certainly hope they are still hiring."

"Sure are, they seem to take on everyone who applies, young and old alike. Maybe too young, if you ask me. But that's between us, they're good customers and I don't want any trouble."

Fletcher nodded. "Sure."

"That's hard and dirty work you're after," Bert went on. "Have you ever worked in a mine before?"

"No sir," Fletcher said, "I have not. I'm just a farmer by trade. But, I'm young, strong and willing to work hard."

"Have you got any family here?" Bert asked.

"No," Fletcher said sadly. "Not yet. My wife will join me soon. I can't convince my parents to come."

Bert nodded and offered his hand. "My wife and I wish you all the best."

"Is there someone who could give me a lift to the work camp?" Fletcher asked.

Eloise was eavesdropping and looking for an opportunity to jump into the conversation. "Our oldest son, Johnny can take you, but it will cost twenty cents. That's his going rate."

"That will be fine." Fletcher said. "Can you supply me? You probably know better than I do what I should purchase."

What a nice young man, Eloise thought. She got an old feed sack and began to fill it up for him. "I hope you will be staying with someone who can cook. You'll need about twenty pounds of flour, lard, three dozen eggs, and three pounds of coffee. I suggest you take a couple pounds of sausage, a pound of bacon and two pounds of sugar."

"That's fine, ma'am. I trust your experience. I don't want to show up empty handed."

Bert was excitedly jotting down the list and punching the amounts into his new cash register. It might well be their biggest ticket of the day! With a loud ding, the machine calculated a total. "That'll be a dollar ninety-eight," Bert told him. He hoped Fletcher had some money. If not, he would start an account for him. That's how most miners handled their shopping.

Fletcher let out a soft whistle. That was a big sum, but he reminded himself that this was a month's supply of groceries. He counted out the money.

Bert told him, "Once you get on at the mines, you might find you need some tools. Some are supplied, but many of the miners have their own. You might need a shovel, pick, hoe and a wedge. We carry all those items, but I suggest you wait and see exactly what you need, if anything."

Eloise went to the stairs and called to her son, Johnny. He came bounding down the steps. He was a tall gangly boy and badly in need of a haircut. His blonde hair stuck out in all directions.

Johnny quickly loaded the groceries into the wagon, hitched the horse and they got underway. Fletcher was astonished to see a motorized vehicle go smoking and sputtering past them, spooking the horse slightly. The friendly driver, a man with a leather hat and goggles, waved a cheery hello as he sped past.

Johnny commented, "Only the rich people around here have one of those vehicles. There are only about six or seven in town. One family has two! I think they are ridiculous, like some big toy for grownups."

Fletcher thought he detected just a hint of jealously in Johnny's lament. But he said nothing, of course.

A soft snow was starting to fall again. "It's going to be another cold night," Johnny told Fletcher, and Fletcher thought, *Son, you have no idea what cold is.* Tonight Johnny would be all snuggled in at his warm home and Fletcher would be sleeping in a tent. He shivered at the thought.

They clopped along the dirt street through town. After about a half mile, they turned left onto a rougher dirt road that stretched out as far as Fletcher could see.

"The camp is just a couple of miles down here on the left," Johnny said.

They rode along in silence for a bit. Fletcher noticed a spattering of little houses along the way with smoke curling out of their chimneys. His eyes took in the rolling countryside with the beautiful mountain views. He wasn't sure how far the river was from the campsite. He thought the men said it was fairly close by. He was looking forward to doing a little fishing. Yes, this looked like it was going to be a good place to call home.

"No one ever has any problem out of your folks, but those I-talian fellows are always making trouble and getting into fights like they've got something to prove," Johnny said.

Fletcher noticed Johnny used a long "I" intonation on the word Italian. "I'm just looking for a job, not trouble."

"Sometimes, trouble finds you whether you're looking for it or not."

"Well, let's hope not. I can usually get along with folks. I'd like to think that will continue," Fletcher told the young man. "You haven't had any problem with those I-talians have you, Johnny?"

"No sir. My dad says they're hot blooded and alright unless they've been drinking sour mash."

Fletcher laughed out loud. "Probably true of most folks. I've never much cared for liquor and I hope you don't develop a taste for it either."

While Fletcher enjoyed being off his feet for the short ride to the work camp, he couldn't help but worry some about the money it had cost him. His friends would think him frivolous spending his money this way. Fletcher would think of this as an early Christmas gift to himself this year. He certainly hadn't wasted too much money getting here.

Arriving at the camp, he noticed very few people milling around, mostly older family members and a few womenfolk with small children. It was a Tuesday afternoon and most of the men were probably hard at work, earning a living.

He thanked Johnny for bringing him to the site. He asked around and discovered which tent belonged to his two friends, Clyde and

Rodger. He carried the supplies into their tent. He noticed his friends'
pantry area looked nearly depleted. Well, he was glad he could begin
to earn his keep.

He walked around the camp a little introducing himself to the
folks there. He asked if there was anything he could help them with.
Everyone seemed hospitable, but didn't need any help.

Fletcher went back to his tent, grabbed one of the woolen blankets
folded up in the corner and, covering himself with it, fell fast asleep
in the middle of the afternoon.

CHAPTER 12

A Miner's Life

For the Scripture says, "You shall not muzzle an ox while it treads out the grain, and, "The laborer is worthy of his wages.

I Timothy 5:18

Clyde and Rodger were surprised to find someone sleeping in their tent when they arrived home. It was dark and when they lit the lantern there was a man huddled in one of their blankets. They were both covered in coal dust. Fletcher woke at the sound of them coming into the tent.

He sat up. He couldn't believe how dark it was outside or how very strange his friends looked. All he could make out were the whites of their eyes and their teeth in their smiling mouths.

"We had about given up on you, Fletch," said Clyde.

"How was your trip?" Rodger asked. "I can't imagine how rough traveling this time of year must've been."

"I can't even begin to tell you how glad I am to finally get here," Fletcher said. "It must have been around two when I got to camp. I guess sleeping so long is a sure sign of just how tired I was."

"You better catch up on your rest while you can," said Clyde. "It feels like we just get home, wash up, at least our faces and hands," he grinned. "Then we eat a bite, hit the sack and start it all over again the next morning."

Rodger looked at the food Fletcher had brought and said, "Unless you happen to be some type of fantastic cook, what we usually do is go over and have our meals with the Henderson family. You remember Peter Henderson? He's a little older than us. His mother and father are here. They've taken all us single guys under their wing. We just help supply the groceries."

Fletcher said, "That sounds like a plan to me. I can hardly boil water, but coming over on the ship, I got pretty good at peeling potatoes."

"Let's head on over there," said Clyde.

The two men quickly washed up and left the tent with Fletcher. They helped carry Fletcher's new food supply over to Mrs. Henderson. She had a big kettle of German sauerkraut and dumplings cooked up for them. There was also hot coffee. The men typically just had meat a couple times a week, usually on Sunday, when the mines were closed, and about midweek, depending on supplies.

Fletcher didn't realize how hungry he was until Mrs. Lola Henderson handed him a heaping plate of food. They were perfectly seasoned, just the way he remembered.

"Thank you ma'am," he said. "These taste just like my Mama's. This is the best meal I've had since I left Germany."

Mrs. Henderson beamed at his praise. "There is plenty to go around. I tell you, we don't always have much variety, but I try to make sure it's good and hot. And just so you know, I will be packing a lunch for you, too. You need to get one of those lunch pails to keep your food clear of all that coal dust."

The other men present felt somewhat sheepish. Their diet did consist of fairly routine meals and maybe they had been taking the good food Mrs. Henderson prepared for them for granted. And yes, there might even have been some growling about the same old stuff again. Clyde and Rodger agreed that the next time they went into town they needed to pick up something special for her. Maybe a new apron.

The men cleared out of the Henderson tent and headed back to their own quarters. They had enough canvas to double-cover their tent. It was fastened at the bottom with stakes and the door could be kept securely closed. It was big enough for the grown men to stand up in.

They sat up that night talking about their families and plans to reunite. Clyde had been working about nine months and was getting close to having enough for his family's passage. He had a young son and daughter. Rodger was single, but hoping to bring his mother and father to America. They all bemoaned the fact that it took so long to receive mail between the two countries.

They settled in to get some rest. The whistle blast would sound around six in the morning and they would be expected to be at the mine by seven-thirty. Right now they were working twelve hour days. It was agreed that Fletcher would ride in with them the next morning and meet the mine boss.

Clyde and Rodger were considered experienced miners now. They were making two dollars a day. They warned Fletcher that he couldn't expect to make those wages just starting out, but to be firm that he needed at least a dollar fifty. There were teenagers working there who were getting anywhere from seventy-five cents to a dollar a day depending on their experience and size. Fletcher was a grown man; he needed to ask for more.

Fletcher lay awake thinking over all they had told him. He had never negotiated for his pay. That sounded awkward. After all, he was thrilled to get on at the mines. He wondered if his friend's advice was wise. A dollar and a half a day sounded awfully good to him, but maybe more than he was worth.

When the whistle blast sounded the next morning, everyone seemed to go into overdrive. Fletcher thought he would get run over. He did his best to stay out of the way. He and his friends went to the

Henderson tent. There, they had apple butter biscuits and more coffee for breakfast. Their lunch for the day was baked bean sandwiches and some fried carrots, still warm. *That old girl must get up at dawn to fix for them all*, Fletcher thought.

He was by far the cleanest man in the wagon headed to the mine. He noticed his friends' fingernails were black. He stared down at his own. He thought he better take a good look because he might not see them looking like that anytime soon.

It was a blue cold morning. The men were huddled against one another as much for warmth as necessity. Fletcher got his first look at the crooked and narrow road leading to the mine. The light snow made the passage a little slippery, but the tired-looking horse pressed on. The road had a number of ruts and they were jostled about in the wagon. Fletcher thought it amazing that none of them was pitched over the side of the wagon on the rough road.

When they reached the mine entrance, Fletcher's eyes took in the operation. He hadn't realized that there was so much modernization involved in the process. It looked carefully thought-out and very systematic. He watched as the trolley system was being prepared to bring the coal back to the surface. Mules strained to pull the bizarre looking little train. It was easy to see why those animals were called beasts of burden. The young boys taking care of the mules looked mighty young to Fletcher. If he had to guess, he thought they might be twelve or thirteen. That surprised him.

His friends took him directly to meet the foreman. The rough looking fellow seemed too preoccupied to take much notice of him. When they finally got his attention, he gave Fletcher an once-over and told him, "You'll do."

Fletcher wasn't sure what he meant by that, but his friends nudged him in the ribs with their elbow and waited alongside expectantly.

"Sir, do you mean I am hired?" Fletcher cautiously asked.

"Are you smart or something?" the big foreman sneered. "Yes, you've been offered a job. Now, if you aren't interested, then be off with you, I have work to do."

Fletcher gulped audibly. "No sir. No disrespect. I've just arrived here in America. I'm not so good with the language yet. I'm interested in the job. May I ask you how much I will be paid?

The foreman studied the broad-chested young man for a long moment. "I'll give you a dollar a day until I can see what you can do."

Fletcher managed to say, "I'm grateful for the offer, but I couldn't possibly work for that. I have to bring my family over."

The other two men braced themselves for the onslaught of cursing Fletcher had probably just heaped on himself. They kept their eyes averted and didn't meet the foreman's eyes.

Sarcasm dripped from the foreman's words when he spoke. "So, just how much do you think your time is worth, young man?"

Fletcher spoke quietly. "A dollar and a half a day," he said. "I'll pull my weight."

The foreman crossed his arms and frowned. After a time, he said, "I'll give you that, but I'll be watching you right close. If I see you slacking, I'll bump you back to a dollar, and you don't say a word. Deal?"

Fletcher's was so excited, or relieved, he couldn't tell which emotion was the dominant one. It felt like his heart would pound right out of his chest. "Yes sir. Thank you."

The foreman had already turned away, his business completed. Fletcher's friends heartily congratulated him.

Clyde said, "I was worried there for a minute, Fletcher. I thought you were going to buckle about the money."

Rodger chimed in, "I know I told you to ask for your fair wage, but I didn't know if we had told you wrong or not. I would have felt awful if you hadn't gotten a job."

"I'm just glad that's over," Fletcher said.

He bowed his head and offered up a silent prayer to the Lord for blessing him with this work. He had no illusions about the work being easy. He thought of the tired look in the eyes of the men around both the breakfast table this morning and as they climbed out of the wagons to begin another day in that long dark hole.

As Fletcher began his first day in the mines, he realized that much, if not all, of his first paycheck or would probably go for gear he needed for the job. Bert was right. He needed a pick, a short handled shovel, a wedge, heavier gloves and a hard helmet complete with carbide light. For now, he would make do with his knit cap and woolen gloves.

By the end of the day, he had already torn a hole in one of the gloves Rachel had knitted for him. His back ached from bending over in the more shallow halls of the mine. He'd survived his first day in the dusty environment and was certain dinner would taste like coal dust too.

It was an exhausted and dirty group of fellows climbing back up into the wagon that night. Fletcher knew he could do the job. Each day of work brought him that much closer to having his family here, and that was good enough for him.

Mrs. Henderson had a delicious dinner prepared for them that evening when they got home. She served up fried potatoes with onions seasoned with plenty of salt and pepper, huge fried hamburger patties which were prepared with an onion, green pepper, day old bread and an egg mixture. They didn't have meat every day, so this was a real treat. She had also made them large biscuits.

Both Clyde and Rodger got letters from their families this week and read them aloud in the tent. Letters from home were a treasure. Fletcher was happy for them, but it did make him long for his family.

Later that day, Fletcher finally managed to get his letters posted to his wife and family. Now they would have his address and could write him. He couldn't wait to hear back from them now that they knew how to reach him. What news would Rachel have about the boys? If they wrote him right away, he might receive their letters by April or May. It seemed like forever, but any word from them would be good. He drifted off to sleep thinking of his little family and missing them all.

CHAPTER 13

Letters Home

The righteous man walks in his integrity; His children are blessed after him.

Proverbs 20:7

As the postman walked along the dusty road to Rachel's house, he thought of the young family that lived there. In his sack he had three letters from a foreign land. From Fletcher. He knew this would be a special day for them, to finally hear from her husband and the children's father. Fletcher had been gone for months and this would be the first evidence to them all that he was safe. He couldn't help but grin. That was the thing about this job; you never knew what kind of news you were delivering. Today, however, these three envelopes made him feel like a hero.

So much time had passed without any word from her husband. She had written several letters to him but didn't know where to mail them. She would have to wait until he reached his work camp and could give her a mailing address.

Her boys were in the yard playing. It was a cold, clear day. She had bundled them up and sent them outdoors to run off some of their nervous energy. Little boys just weren't meant to be cooped up all day. She was hoping that if they played outside for a bit, then when they came in, she could feed them some of the hot vegetable soup she was making and get them down for a good long nap.

She suddenly heard them both yelping like excited puppies. When she looked out her living room window, they were both running down the lane towards the house. She saw the mailman's retreating back in the distance. The boys had something in their hands.

"Momma, Momma!" Joseph shouted. "We have some letters from Daddy!"

"Read them to us, Momma, can you read them to us now?" Arwood begged.

Rachel felt terribly selfish. Her thoughts were to feed them lunch and get them down for a nap while she leisurely read every word in each letter with her swollen ankles propped up and a steaming mug of tea in her hand. She put her arms around her boys and hugged them tightly to her rotund belly.

Joseph laughed. "Momma, the baby is kicking me again!"

He was right. And, she too, could feel the unborn child stirring. Maybe, the baby could sense the excitement produced by the letters from its Daddy.

Rachel said to the boys, "You know how special it is when Papa brings us over his chocolate? What do we do?"

Joseph said, "I know, Momma! We just have one piece and save the rest of it for later."

"That's right, Joseph. Let's do that with this special treat too. I'm going to open the letters this afternoon after you both take your nap. There are three of them, let's count, one, two, three… but you know what? There's a big mystery here!"

Little Arwood piped up, "What is a mistwee, Momma?"

Joseph joined in, "The mailman said they looked like letters from our Daddy." He said in a worried, questioning tone.

"They are, Joseph. Now Arwood, a mystery means something we just don't know yet. Something we have to figure out."

The boys looked at each other knowingly. Momma sure was acting funny.

"What we don't know is which one to open first. Which one did Daddy write first? When I read you a story, you know how you want me to start at the beginning and read it all the way until it says…"

"The end!" they both shouted.

"So, when we open them, like one of your stories you love, we don't to read the middle first, then the beginning and then the end, do we?"

Joseph said, "No Momma, we want you to read them all to us, the right way."

"Well, you know what? I have to look for a clue so we know which one to read first."

Joseph said, "Momma, we don't know what a clue is."

"I think Daddy put something on all the letters so we know which one to read first, second and third," she explained.

The boys looked puzzled. "What did he put on them?" Joseph asked.

"I think when we open each letter; we will see a date that means which day he wrote the letter. Then, all we have to do is read the first date, the second date and then the last date! After supper tonight, we will have some hot chocolate and I will read the first letter to you. How does that sound?"

The boys were covering her with hugs and kisses. "Now, go wash your hands and faces and get ready for lunch."

They both scampered off to do as she asked.

While the boys napped, Rachel opened the letters and placed them in date order and wrote the date on the outside of each envelope and reinserted the letters into the envelopes. It was February and this was really a perfect if late Christmas gift from her husband. She would read only the first letter today so as to give herself something to look forward to.

19 September, 1919

My Dear Rachel,

I have found that I have what they call "sea legs." I hope you and the boys have some, too. I guess I'd better explain…it seems that many folks have the misfortune of having their stomachs turn against them when they embark on a ship ride. We have been blessed with smooth sailing the ship hands tell me. Evidently, it is not uncommon for storms to blow up in autumn and make the going rougher on everyone, crew and passengers alike.

I want you to know that I was so impressed with the big city of Hamburg. I found it somewhat overwhelming, but the people were friendly and helpful.

I know that I want to save a little extra so that the first night you are here, you can afford to stay at one of the Inns with the children. It's fine for me to rough it, I'm a man, but I certainly wouldn't want that for my family.

I'm a little uncomfortable telling you the nature of the work I'm doing aboard this big tub. I thought I might be hoisting sails, pitching coal in the steamer's furnace or other such manly endeavors, but that is not the case. It seems that the good captain has seen fit to install me in the kitchen! I'm doing very little cooking as it is. Mostly, my work consists of hauling vegetables and barrels of grain to the Cook, Claude, washing dishes, stowing the dishes, mopping the floors, cleaning the tables and occasionally peeling potatoes, skinning onions and the likes.

Not really what I would call a man's work, but here's the best part-they're paying me to do this job and my bunk and meals are included! I feel truly blessed because now I can save the money I expected to pay for my fare and food to put towards our future.

I hope the boys are behaving themselves. Please tell them I love them and can't wait to see them again. They are the joy of my life and I miss my boys!

Joseph, are you taking care of your dog? Remember, he needs fresh water every day. I'm just counting the hours and days until I have you all back with me. I miss you and love you all with all my heart,

Yours Always,

Fletcher

Rachel read and re-read the letter. She smiled to herself thinking of Fletcher working in a kitchen. Somehow, that was a hard thing to imagine. But he sounded happy.

He had never been away from home, or her and the children, and she had worried that he might become depressed or homesick. It was early enough that it was still a great adventure for him.

The boys tore through. They were so anxious to hear Momma read the letter from their father.

They laughed and laughed when she read the part about their Daddy having "sea legs." They had heard stories about sea monsters and octopuses. They could imagine their Daddy with those kinds of legs. They aped around the living room acting like they too had all those legs, and Rachel couldn't help laughing.

They talked about the big ship on which their Daddy had sailed. Just being boys, they longed to see the huge boat. They didn't quite know what to think about their father working in the kitchen. Rachel explained that the ship's kitchen made food for hundreds of people. She described their big strong daddy lifting and carrying heavy barrels of dried beans, big sacks of potatoes and onions, not the jars or little bowls of vegetables they got from their cellar.

She talked to them about how he had been able to save his money and was making even more money by working so hard. That would mean he would soon have enough money for them all to go to America and be with him. The boys cheered and their little hearts swelled with pride for their Daddy. Momma said he was on a big adventure.

She got them ready for bed and read them a story. Joseph looked at his father's picture and somehow, tonight, Daddy didn't seem so far away. He liked hearing Momma read Daddy's words, especially the part about them being the joy of his life and how he missed them. He loved his Daddy and missed him too. They both drifted off to sleep before Rachel could finish the storybook.

The next morning when Rachel awoke, she picked up the second of Fletcher's letters. She took her cup of coffee and sat in the living room by the window. Watching the sunrise, she unfolded the crisp, thin paper and began to read.

14 October, 1919

My Dear Rachel,

I have now been on this ship for over a month. We continue to have fair weather for sailing. I have had you and the boys on my mind so much lately. I know you have no way to reach me on this ship, but I can't help but worry about you all. I have you in my prayers. I have asked the Lord to watch over you while we are apart from one another. We should be arriving in America in about five to six weeks if all goes well.

I imagine the weather is starting to get a little cooler there. After that long, hot Summer, it's probably a welcome relief to have a little cool air. I just hope we have enough wood stacked up to get you all through the Winter.

Have you been over to visit with Mama and Papa? When I saw my Papa last, I watched him driving away in the wagon and wondered if that would be the last time I ever saw him. I have to tell you that was a very bad feeling, do you think we will ever be able to talk them into joining us in America? Papa wouldn't have to work in the mines, we could all live together and he could help take care of the farm.

How are you and the boys making out on your own? I hope the children aren't being too difficult for you to manage. Have you all forgotten me yet? Tonight when you put them to bed, give them a special hug from their Daddy. And while you're at it, give yourself one too.

Yours Always,

Fletcher

She felt tears trickle down her cheeks. What a lovely, thoughtful man her husband was, always thinking of her and the children.

That night, when she read the second letter from Daddy, Joseph was oddly quiet.

Rachel said, "Joseph, what's the matter?"

His little face looked so sad, it broke Rachel's heart. "Momma, do you think Mama and Papa are going to stay here and not go on the ship with all of us?"

Rachel answered him honestly, "Son, we don't know. But we hope they will change their minds and come with us."

She looked at Arwood. He was playing quietly with his toys and not paying much attention to their conversation. That night when she put them to bed and went through their bedtime story, they lay quietly in the bed but didn't go right to sleep. Rachel turned off the lantern. She kissed them both goodnight and delivered that extra hug from their daddy.

Rachel went about the house slowly tidying up things. It was quiet and she heard little boy voices coming from the tiny bedroom. She listened at the door.

In a hushed tone, Joseph said, "Arwood, are you asleep?"

Arwood yawned and said, "I'm awake."

"I think Daddy is sad because Mama and Papa don't want to go with us," he told his little brother.

"Are you sad too because they don't want to come with us? I am. It's not fair." Joseph complained to his little brother.

"We won't get any more cookies," Arwood said. "Momma doesn't like to make cookies."

"Yeah," said Joseph, "No more cookies."

"I want more cookies," Arwood said, sniffling.

Rachel almost giggled. She loved their talks. They didn't happen very often, but when they did, it was usually about something very important. Like cookies.

She prepared for bed and prayed that wherever her husband was that he was safe and warm. She couldn't wait to see him again. There was just one more letter to read. Knowing that made Rachel both anxious and just a little sad. How long would it be before she heard from him again? She decided to save the next letter for after lunch tomorrow. *No peeking*, she promised herself.

For lunch the next day, Rachel fried them all a pork chop, made tiny little biscuits and served some of her canned applesauce with cinnamon. She and the boys enjoyed a steaming mug of hot chocolate too. She put them down for a short nap.

Tonight, they were going over to stay with Mama and Papa. She needed to have some time to finish knitting them all new hats, mittens and scarves. She was going to read the third letter from their Daddy to them before they got picked up this evening. But first, she prepared to see the message her husband had written to them all. Curling her feet up under her, she opened the last letter.

21 November, 1919

My Dear Rachel,

The captain expects to reach New York City in a matter of days. I'm beginning to wish I had been wise enough to ask more questions of our friends who have already settled here. From talking with others on the ship, many plan to take the railroad to points south. There is a train line in a state called Pennsylvania that goes directly to Roanoke Virginia. That would put me very close to Montgomery County and the McCoy area there. If I had to walk from Roanoke, it may take me a good 2-3 days. So it's probable that I will be in McCoy the week before Christmas. That will be something to celebrate.

The air has a definite bite to it right now. I suspect that this climate is very similar to what you are experiencing in Germany. I trust you have everything you need, plenty of food and wood to keep the house warm? I will miss celebrating Christmas with you and our family. We haven't been apart for Christmas since we met. It will be a little blue here with you way over there.

I will post these letters as soon as I arrive in Virginia. I can't wait to hear from you. Praying you are all happy and healthy. I am missing you with every breath I take. You and the children are my everything. Please tell the boys I love them and Merry Christmas from their Daddy.

Yours Always,

Fletcher

Rachel knew that these letters had been posted at least eight to ten weeks ago. Mail coming from the States was so slow and came via ocean vessels. It seemed to take forever for letters to gradually work their way to her doorstep. The sad part was that by the time she received Fletcher's letter telling her where to write him, it would be almost time to pack her and the family for their trip over. She could just hand deliver her letters. She might have time to get them off to him before his family arrived. Time was creeping and rushing for her all at the same time.

The boys would think it funny that their daddy was wishing them Merry Christmas in February. They had enjoyed this last holiday season in their little home. There had been lots of good food and a Christmas party at Mama and Papa's. Rachel's dad had joined them. She and the boys had managed to put up a little Christmas tree. Her father had insisted that she use the beautiful ornaments her mother and he had collected over the years. The old dear had wrapped them in thick, white butcher paper, tied a beautiful ribbon around the package and presented them as his gift to her family. Rachel had cried as she opened the box later and removed the decorations one by one. She recalled the many holidays she had celebrated with both her Mom and Dad. It had now been three years since her mother had died. Rachel still thought about her and still missed her mother.

She re-read all the letters from Fletcher. The house was particularly warm this afternoon. She was so comfortable in the big stuffed chair. In no time, she fell fast asleep while her children napped in the next room.

CHAPTER 14

A Good Day

May the God of hope fill you with all joy and peace as you trust in him, so that you may overflow with hope by the power of the Holy Spirit.

Romans 15:13

Hilda awoke that freezing February day sorely missing Fletcher. It was a deep yearning which was really more than mere words could express. She thought it most akin to mothers sending their sons off to war. They must experience a deep sense of hope, anxiety and even pride. Mothers had to entrust the world to love their child as they loved them, to keep them free from harm. But, it was more than that. It was the knowledge deep down in your heart that you may never see their child again, that he might be lost to you.

It was not as if she loved her youngest child any more than her oldest son, Peter. Hilda knew she was probably being foolish in her fear, but a Momma needs to lay her eyes on her child from time to time. He was her last baby after all.

Bless John's heart; he had done his level best to reassure her that Fletcher was having a grand adventure in that new country. Hilda didn't believe a word of it. And, she figured John was just better at hiding his emotions than she. How could he not be concerned and still love his son? Well, it just wasn't possible as far as she was concerned. What was his life like aboard the ship she wondered? She had heard gruesome tales about the rough nature of ship crews. What if he had been killed by one of those black hearts? Hot tears flooded her eyes. The not knowing was the hardest part. Why was it that when a mother didn't know something, her mind immediately went to the worst possible outcome? She recalled the bible verse in Romans 8:27: *And he who searches our hearts knows the mind of the Spirit, because the Spirit intercedes for God's people in accordance with the will of God.*

More to occupy her mind than anything else, she set about preparing dinner. Today, she was going to make a simple *lobscouse.* Her pork roast had been slowly baking since daybreak and should be nice and tender by now. She tested it with her fork and liked the way it gently pulled apart. *Perfect,* she thought.

She carefully peeled and coarsely cut up potatoes, onion, turnips and celery. Her family were true potato lovers. She could do no wrong provided she was always heavy-handed on the potatoes in her simple recipes. Her stew would soon be underway. Removing her pork roast from the oven, she emptied the rich, flavorful broth into her big metal kettle that had been her mother's and cranked up the heat so the vegetables could tenderize. Many a family meal had nourished the family from this kettle. Hilda proceeded to cut the savory pot roast into large chunks. Then she seasoned the stew with a little sage, rosemary and thyme, kosher salt, pepper and her secret ingredient: about a quarter cup of raw sugar. She covered the kettle and let it simmer.

Earlier in the day, she had baked bread and wrapped it in linen cloth to keep it moist. When her meal was cooked just the way she wanted it, she would thickly slice the bread, top it with a thin wedge of cheddar cheese and place it back in the oven just long enough to warm the bread and melt the cheese. They would feast all weekend on this dish and when it got thin, she would do a few side dishes to stretch it out. Hilda had yet to learn the art of cooking a small meal. Not that John ever complained.

Tomorrow was Saturday and she would invite Doctor Smyth and his wife to join them for a meal after church. He and his wife were like most folks in town: they eked out a living. Many of his patients paid him in kind which meant meat, vegetables, eggs, cheese or some of their canned goods. Times were hard and, as her mother might have said, they were likely to get harder before they got better.

John and Peter had been out cutting down trees most of the day. They were fortunate to have acres and acres of woods on their property. On this cold evening, they would welcome a nice, hot meal. She had already told her daughter-in-law, Karen, to plan to have dinner with them tonight. She and Peter had been married for nearly eight years. Karen had lost two babies and the midwife had told her it would be dangerous for her to become pregnant again. The first one she lost had been at three months and the second, just past the fourth.

All of them doted on Rachel and Fletcher's children, but none more so than Karen and Peter. Hilda accepted that Karen's motherhood opportunities were behind her. That didn't erase the deep melancholy and longing in that girl for a child of her own to love and nurture. But Karen had so much love to give. Fletcher's two little rascals received a full dose of that love and attention.

After enjoying a quick breakfast, John and Peter had left out at first light. Hilda had packed them a bagged lunch which she hoped didn't freeze. Peter had hitched both horses to the two wagons, so they could capitalize on this sunny but brisk day. There had been a number of harsh storms this winter. John never felt too comfortable when he saw his woodpile going down.

The biting air had chapped their cheeks and noses. John was just thankful the wind had died down. He thought back over the years of cutting wood and raising his two boys. Last year, Fletcher had tried his best to convince John to let Peter and him take over this chore. Truth be told, he looked forward to this time alone with them. There were times when men needed to just be out working with other men, no womenfolk around. Times when they could just get things done without any interference, without a lot of conversation, times they could just burp right out loud if they felt like it and tell tales and lies. John grinned to himself.

He and Peter had felled three good sized trees. His old woolen gloves had been patched multiple times. They were his favorites for working the two man crosscut saw with the sharp tuttle teeth. They allowed him to get a good firm grip on the smooth wooden handle. If they maintained their focus, they might be able to get one of those fine timbers cut, split, chopped and loaded into the wagons before evening. His plan was to deliver at least half a load to Rachel and the boys the next day. They kept her well stocked.

As usual, John and Peter had brought their guns just in case they saw any game on the way back. Personally, John was hoping for a turkey or two, but he knew Peter wanted to spot a deer. His wife made the most delicious stew using venison, stewed tomatoes, red beans, green peppers, onions, garlic and chili powder (if they could secure it). Along with the stew, she usually served up corn pones and a big pan of salty fried potatoes. Yes, they definitely needed to keep the women of the family, those good cooks, warm and supplied with plenty of wood for their cook stoves.

They worked steadily with just a short break for lunch. As much as John hated to admit it, his son might be right. This was young man's work. They finished up the tree in the late afternoon and headed back home.

John's back, hands and arms ached from the daylong exertion in the brisk air. He would pay for this later, he knew. He dreamed of a hot bath and, if he was lucky, Hilda might give him a backrub after his bath tonight.

He worried about Rachel being alone with that new baby on the way. He and Hilda were hoping for a girl. He had two boys and then along came Fletcher with two of his own. There was nothing wrong with having boys to carry on the family name, but he thought it would be nice to have a little granddaughter.

He smiled. Fletcher going to be in for a surprise when Rachel and the boys joined him in America. Fletcher left before Rachel was certain she was expecting. John thought she probably had a good suspicion, like most women seemed to. If she knew, she kept it to herself. One thing was certain, though: if Fletcher had known, he would never have left her. That boy worshipped his wife and family.

When they crested the hill, John watched the beautiful reflection of the trees and hillside in the large pond below. Then John's heart soared. In front of them was a whole rafter of wild turkeys. They were fatted up for winter. He signaled to Peter and they quietly got down from their wagons. They managed to shoot three before the hens flew to safety.

When they reached the house, he caught a glimpse of Hilda through the kitchen window. She was pacing back and forth. Wonder what was worrying her? His first thought was that something was wrong with Rachel or his grandsons. But then he knew that couldn't be. She would be over there, not here.

He stiffly got down from wagon and asked Peter to put up the horses. He hurried inside. His trepidation proved to be in vain. When Hilda heard him enter the house, she let out an excited whoop, ran over and hugged his neck.

"What is it, Hildie?"

"Oh John, finally, finally we have a couple of letters from Fletcher! It took everything I had to not open the letters before you got home."

He sat down at their little kitchen table. "Let's share a hot cup of coffee and read what our boy has to say. Just let me send Peter home to get cleaned up for dinner. We'll unload the wood later. We managed to get a few turkeys today. I'm going to put them in the well house."

Hilda's smile dimmed a little. "So, we have to wait until supper to read them?"

"No ma'am. We will let Peter and Karen see them later, but for now, they are for our eyes only, my dear."

While he went outside to speak to Peter, Hilda put on some coffee to brew. She checked on her stew. As she did these things, she quietly prayed. "Thank you our Heavenly Father, for all your many blessings. You know how these letters have cheered this mother's heart don't you Lord? All these months had left me so worried about my son. Forgive me Lord for not trusting you more. You have answered my prayers and kept my son safe. I praise your Holy Name! No matter what words are inside these envelopes, I know my son has made it to America. Please be with him. Teach me patience and to trust you more each day of my life. Amen."

John stoked the fire and Hilda poured the steaming coffee into their two mugs. Taking out his pocket knife, he expertly split the envelope tops. He recognized his son's neat scrawl and pictured in his mind, his son as he addressed the letters to them. The first letter was dated in September and the second one nearly one month later in October.

He took a long sip of the strong, hot coffee, cleared his throat and began to read the first letter aloud to his wife.

22 September, 1919

Dear Mama and Papa,

Just wanted to let you know that I had a safe journey to Hamburg. I met some interesting, but good people, along the way who were all very helpful to me. That city was something else. I'd never seen so many people in one place. I guess you could say, I got a chance to see how the wealthy people live too. One of the things that I have learned being on this ship is that the more money folks have, the ruder they are to people they consider beneath them, me included. If that is how having money makes people act, I'll just remain poor, thank you.

How are you and Papa doing? Please don't worry about me. I'm doing fine except for the fact that the captain has me working in the kitchen. Can you imagine, big strong me, a kitchen hand? The Cook is a character named Claude. He likes that I'm a hard worker who doesn't complain and gets my work done. Go ahead and tell my brother what I'm doing, he will laugh his head off. But also, tell him this...they are paying me, giving me my meals and a bunk to sleep in. I didn't have to use any of the money I saved up for this trip. Praise the Lord for his provision. That will get me that much closer to getting Rachel and children over here with me. I miss them and you two terribly.

All My Love,

Fletcher

They both laughed at the thought of Fletcher helping in the kitchen. That boy didn't know where to begin to be useful in a kitchen. Oh my, they joked about him being tossed overboard for ruining dinner. He was right; his brother was going to guffaw over that little tidbit of information.

20 October, 1919

Dear Mama and Papa,

Time seems to be flying aboard this ship. I had imagined that the trip might seem boring and long. The Cook keeps me so busy, I can't see straight. By the time I finish up all the chores, it's time for me to turn in and start it all over again the next morning. I can't really say I've learned a thing about cooking other than the fact it makes some people cantankerous!

We're past the halfway mark on this trip. Soon, I'll be in the company of people I know again. It will be good to see so many folks from our little village again. I'm going to try to bunk with a couple of the guys. I understand they are all living in tents for the most part. That should be very interesting this Winter. I think I already miss our nice stove and warm house.

I'm hoping you both will keep an open mind about coming to America and staying with us. As soon as I'm able, I'm going to try to purchase a little acreage, enough for all of us to build a house on.

Please watch after Rachel and the boys for me. I miss you.

All My Love,

Fletcher

They reached across the table and held hands as tears streaked unashamedly down their cheeks.

CHAPTER 15

Missing Fletcher

May your unfailing love be with us, Lord, even as we put our hope in you.

Psalm 33:22 (TNIV)

It was an unseasonably warm day in April. Rachel had just washed her family's laundry in the stream by the house. The water felt deliciously cool and lightened her mood towards the task. A bead of sweat cruised down her face. She wrung all their clothing piece by piece, twisting and squeezing out the fresh water, placing them in the waiting basket. Rachel's brow and hair were damp from the exertion. Her bulging belly made this normally simple task a much bigger challenge.

Fletcher should be receiving her letter soon, letting him know that they had a new baby on the way. What a surprise those letters would be for him, what with news of the baby. And the letter from his parents informing him that they were coming to America, too. It was just a matter of them getting the house sold and Rachel getting on her feet after childbirth. When the midwife examined her, she told Rachel that the baby should be arriving early May. It wouldn't be long now.

Her back ached a little as she walked back towards the house where the boys were, hopefully, still napping. She was determined to keep herself busy to prevent melancholy from setting in. The Lord knew she didn't have to look for work, not with two active little boys to keep her company and a garden to tend.

She and Fletcher often joked that if Arwood had been born first, he might have been an only child. He had deep dimples like his mother and a mischievous spirit that neither of them wanted to claim. His brother, on the other hand, was a calm young boy, even-tempered and slow to become annoyed with his little brother. Arwood loved his big brother and the two were inseparable.

She couldn't help missing Fletcher. Other friends' husbands preceded him and now she had joined the lonely ranks of women waiting to see their loved ones again. For the most part, their friends were able to have their families travel together. As fast as time seemed to be flying, it wouldn't be any time before she could leave with their own little family to join her husband.

Rachel had written Fletcher a letter telling him the exciting news about the new baby. She worried that he would think he had to return right away. She had assured him that she was fine and that when the time came, she would just send for old Mrs. Meyer, the midwife. She felt strong and had managed well during her last two pregnancies.

Despite her best efforts to calm her husband's fears, she knew the new baby on the way would be a worry for him.

Spreading the clothes over the line to dry, Rachel imagined the reunion with him. Her daydreams were cut short by the sound of a squabble between the children. Heading across the yard, she found them making a fuss over their shoes. It seems little Arwood had decided he should wear his big brother's shoes and big brother had other ideas. The things children could find to fuss about!

"Out you go," she said. "It's a lovely day, and you don't even need to wear your shoes. See who can catch a butterfly first. I saw one while I was down at the creek."

The petty argument was quickly forgotten as the two boys' eyes met. They bounded out the door as it slammed behind them. It gave Rachel a moment to think about what to prepare for their supper, but first, she was going to need to tidy up her kitchen.

Staring out her small kitchen window, she watched their two hardy boys. The rambunctious puppy their father had gotten from a man down the road scampered along after them, his tail wagging, determined to keep up. The boys were playing in the sunshine, laughing, running, tumbling around on the front lawn of their modest little home. They had already forsaken the butterfly search.

As she looked about at their meager possessions, she knew that while they were not the best, she would still miss them when it came time to leave. They had already discussed trying to sell what they could before she joined him. Household items were one thing, but what about the memories? Would those travel well?

Why couldn't you just collect all the precious memories and gently pack them away in a satchel? Then, when you wanted absolute recall of the experience, you could just gingerly unpack them and gaze upon them, see the expressions, read the faces, smell the fragrances, hear all the sounds, listen to all the voices, feel all the emotions and the warmth?

What would Rachel want to remember? Their courtship and wedding, the hard work getting this house ready to move into, the birth of their children, her lovely mother, and her children's every expression, the many family gatherings, the wonderful sunrises, the list was endless.

Of course, some folks might have memories they'd just as soon forget. Not her though. Every one of hers and their little family's memories were so precious, she didn't want to leave a single one behind. Yes, there had been a few heated newlywed disagreements as they had learned to live with each other, but even those memories had helped shape who they were today.

With the supper dishes behind her she busied herself with her children. After their baths she trimmed their hair. Rachel marveled at how the locks sprang back into place as she cut them. It seemed impossible to give her boys a bad haircut with hair as forgiving as theirs. And, as much as they squirmed while she was cutting their hair, she needed all the forgiveness she could get.

After their prayers, they scrambled into bed, all grins and sleepy eyes, winding down at last. She read them a story, their favorite, about the little tin soldier. They loved the beautiful pictures in the book. Joseph wanted to look at his father's picture. Sometimes, he fell asleep holding onto the picture. His little brother was already fast asleep and snuggled up against him.

Rachel and Joseph talked about his father. They played a little guessing game about what his father might be doing just now. Joseph rubbed his sleepy eyes and asked, "Mother, do you think Father remembers me?"

"Joseph, your father loves you. He loves us all! It won't be too long before we're all together again." She ruffled his hair and kissed him goodnight. Rachel turned off the light, but left the door ajar so the room would stay warm.

Rachel coped so much better during the day than she did in the evening, when the boys were asleep and the house grew quiet. If not for her faith, she would have gone crazy with her loneliness. She went into the kitchen and prepared herself a cup of tea and put her feet up by the stove and her thoughts turned to her husband.

Rachel felt herself drifting off to sleep and roused herself so she could climb into bed and get some rest. Before going to bed, she put another couple of logs in the stove to keep the house warm for them all. Once the sun had set, the coolness settled in.

From her bed, she looked out the window at the star-drenched sky. What a beautiful night. Rachel pictured her husband looking at the same sky and thinking of them all.

Goodnight, my dear husband. Know that I love you and long for you every morning and night. Thoughts of you are never far from my mind.

CHAPTER 16

Mail!

The father of the righteous will greatly rejoice, And he who begets
a wise child will delight in him.

Proverbs 23:24

After a grueling day in the mines, Fletcher was relieved to get home to his cot in the tent he shared with his two friends. It was a cold wet April. He was sick of the mud and coal dust. He would give anything for a week of pure sunshine. The other two fellows were going to be working over for awhile tonight. They got a little extra pay for the work. Fletcher thought about it, but just couldn't make himself stay any longer. It was strictly voluntary.

He quickly washed up and slipped on a clean cotton shirt. Clean was a relative term these days. Nothing seemed as fresh as the laundry Rachel brought in from the clothesline. His few articles of clothing were always neatly pressed and folded and packed away in the wardrobe for him back home. One of the wives took in laundry for a small reasonable fee. She used lye soap that the ladies made at the camp. Fletcher knew she scrubbed her best on their filthy clothes, but the coal dust seemed to permeate to the very innermost fibers.

Fletcher went by Mrs. Henderson's tent and had some of the good fried cornbread and coffee she had prepared for the men. He thanked her and left from there with a full belly. The rain had stopped, but the sky was still gray.

He stopped by to chat with a couple of the men. One had been injured at the mines the week before and was nursing a sprained ankle. His foot had slipped and he had jammed it under one of the mine trolleys. Thank the Lord it hadn't been moving. His friends had pulled him free.

As Fletcher was walking back towards his tent, one of the older men there at the camp hailed him. "Hey son, hold up. I have something here you are going to want to see."

The gentleman reached in his pouch and pulled out three letters and handed them to Fletcher. One was from his Mama and Papa, and the other two had Rachel's neat handwriting on the envelopes.

Fletcher let out a loud whoop. Several people at nearby tents peered out to see what all the excitement was all about. They saw the letters in the young man's hands and exchanged knowing smiles and nods. A person needed that connection to family. It gave them more reason to hunker down and get the work done so they could bring their families here faster. Once that goal was accomplished, the mining families turned to saving their money to find a homestead of their own.

Fletcher walked towards his tent wanting nothing more than to rip into the letters. He had decided that he would open his parents' letter first and save Rachel's for later.

He had carried a hot cup of coffee back to his tent with him. He stretched out on his cot and began to read.

March 12, 1920

Dear Fletcher,

We were overjoyed to hear from you. Glad you have gotten to the state of Virginia and been able to secure work to support yourself. Your father and I were worried to death about you in that strange land by yourself. Sounds like you are managing just fine and we couldn't be happier for you.

We missed you so much at Christmas especially. We enjoyed spending the holiday with your little family. Your young sons are such a joy to our hearts. We try to go and get them whenever we can manage so Rachel can get some rest and get special projects done. She has been knitting up a storm and doing some beautiful work. We have been so proud of how brave she has been in your absence.

This has been a long and brutal winter, Your father and brother have made sure Rachel has had plenty of firewood and food, including fresh meat for their table. We are all looking forward to spring, more so than I ever recall feeling. I'm sure it is a combination of the weather and not having you with us.

We have made a big decision, son. We have worked out a deal with a new family who has moved to our area. We are going to sell our home place and farm. We are all coming with Rachel to Virginia. Having you gone has been like having our hearts torn out of us. We decided we would only move if your brother would come too, because if not, we would be in the same situation, living there and missing him. We have talked to your brother and Karen and they are excited to be coming too.

We will tell Rachel this Sunday when she and the boys come over for dinner. That means that we will be able to pay the passage fees for all of us including your family. Please start looking around for some land and/or a home for us. We can build if there isn't a home already there. We would love to have our three families each have a home on the land. At first, we might have to share a house until we can build. It's looking like our sale will be completed by mid to late June. Summer will be a good time to come, right?

Well, we hope this news will cheer your heart. We know it's been hard for you to be there by yourself. Don't worry Son; soon, we will all be back together again. Your father and I will still put out the garden like usual. We won't have to bother with all the canning this time around.

We will try to write you at least once more before we finalize our

sale. That letter should have more details or at least as much as we

know at the time. Your father and I have a lot of work to do to get

ourselves ready to come. This is a big step for us, but we both feel

like it is the right thing for us to do.

Our Love,

Mama and Papa

Fletcher couldn't believe what he had just read. His parents' news and generosity caught him completely by surprise. His family was going to be able to come even sooner than he had imagined. His heart used to break a little every time he thought of possibly never seeing them again.

He felt stress just drain off of him. That didn't mean that he wouldn't be working just as hard to provide for his family, but now he could shift his focus. He looked forward to finding a piece of land for them all. He thought of all the beautiful countryside he passed on his way to and from the mines each day. If this weekend was clear, he would see if he could borrow a horse and take a ride around. He certainly knew nothing about real estate, but surely someone could help him if he found the right place.

He bowed his head and silently thanked God for the many blessings that were coming his way. God's provision was overwhelming and so unexpected. Fletcher felt unworthy of such bounty. He praised God even when he didn't have the words to express his feelings of happiness. He had been truly blessed by the letter from his parents. There was nothing more they could have said that would have encouraged and cheered him more this dreary day.

Fletcher got to his feet and went out to see if he could help spell some of the fellows chopping wood for the camp fires. He took his turn and that gave the others a chance to get inside and warm up with a good hot cup of coffee.

Fletcher worked till dusk and the men went tent to tent placing a stack of wood there for each family's use. The rest of the stack was left in a common area. Everyone understood that the wood was available to all as needed. There was a nice family atmosphere here in the German tent community.

Fletcher stretched out on his cot, his hands folded behind his head. He was contemplating opening one of Rachel's letters, but wanted to just relax a while first. Before he knew it he was asleep.

CHAPTER 17

Trouble at the Mine

But those who wait on the LORD Shall renew their strength; They shall mount up with wings like eagles, They shall run and not be weary, They shall walk and not faint.

Isaiah 40:31

He was jolted wide awake by the shrill sound of the mine whistle. It couldn't be morning yet. He looked about their tent. Where was Clyde and Rodger anyway? They should be back by now. He went outside and saw most of the men scrambling onto the wagons or busy hitching or saddling horses.

One of the men shouted, "Fletcher! Grab your shovel and get on the wagon! There's been an accident at the mine!"

Fletcher threw on his jacket, grabbed his gloves and shovel, and sped out the door.

The men on his wagon all looked worried. One fellow had hopped on a horse and headed toward town to get the doctor, just in case.

None of them had ever heard the mine whistle in the evening and they all knew men were working overtime there tonight. Men, who hadn't come home yet. They were all thinking the worst. Fletcher wanted to remain hopeful.

He had a sick feeling in his stomach when he realized that Clyde, Rodger and some other men he knew might still be in the mine. He looked around at the faces riding with him, full of worry and fear. Something like this could happen to any of them.

"Fellows, I'm not preacher or anything like that, but do you mind if I pray for these men?" Fletcher offered.

If he had to put a word on the expression on the men's faces, it would be grateful. Each was lost in their own thoughts about the possibilities and was playing out some fairly gruesome scenarios.

He bowed his head and spoke clearly. "Lord, we don't know what awaits us at the end of this ride tonight. We don't know if our friends are injured or worse, but, we know that you are in charge. We ask that you watch over the men at the mine and also all these men going to help. Keep them safe we pray. Amen."

In no time at all, they were at the mine. The men hustled off the wagon and ran into the dark pit. Lanterns lit the way. The dust was thick. They covered their mouths and noses with their handkerchiefs and trudged inside.

The foreman was shouting to them. "Hurry up, get in here, start shoveling!"

Fletcher didn't like the knowing look on the man's face. They began digging frantically. Some men were digging and yelling out names of the men they suspected were inside.

Fletcher didn't know how long they worked before the foreman raised an arm and said, "Shut up for a minute. I thought I heard something."

They listened too. It sounded like muffled moans and a slight clinking sound. One of the men must be hitting his shovel against another one to help the men trying to locate them.

In minutes, they broke through to a small opening and were peering at seven or eight men jammed into the tight enclosure. They were practically stacked on top of one another with no room to move.

The workers slowly untangled and lifted the miners out of the dark pit. Most were barely conscious; several had broken arms or legs. Rodger was among the first men pulled out. They still hadn't found Clyde.

Rodger said, "Everything happened so fast. Clyde was up ahead of me. Oh Lord, you've got to get him out of here."

Fletcher's heart sank. His muscles ached and he could hardly breathe. How any of them felt physically at the moment wasn't important. They had to find the other three men.

The next two men recovered were carried out on a stretcher. Still no sign of Clyde. Fletcher prayed, "No Lord, no, please let us find him." He looked back and noticed other men with tears streaking down their blackened faces.

One said, "It's no use Fletch, he can't survive this long."

"I can't accept that, we are not giving up. We have to keep going. You can leave if you want to, but I won't leave him in there."

"We have to know, one way or the other. I'm praying he's alive."

They found Clyde fifteen minutes later. His head was bleeding, he wasn't conscious, and his right leg was badly broken just below the knee. A large bone jutted out of his calf. His breathing was ragged and irregular.

The men, quickly and as gently as possible, loaded Clyde onto their makeshift stretcher. The helpers looked at one another sorrowfully. They weren't doctors, but none of them, including Fletcher, held out much hope for this young man.

As they emerged with the last miner, everyone cheered. Fletcher looked about and was surprised to see so many of the women from the camp outside the mine. Some were wives, others were mothers or sisters. They were holding bright torches to light the way. The survivors, those who could walk, were checked by the doctor and released back to camp with orders to take it easy, but they wouldn't leave. They waited to make sure everyone made it out. There was a brotherhood among the men who shared this occupation.

The doctor hurried over and checked Clyde's vitals. "Hurry, fellows. Help get him into the wagon. Grab some blankets. If you don't have any, give me your jackets. We need to keep him warm. I need a couple of you to come with me to help get him into my office. It's going to be a long night."

On the way to town, they stopped by the nurse's house. Fletcher ran up to her door and banged loudly.

The nurse came to the door with her hair up in rollers and a big thick robe wrapped around her. "Ma'am," he said, "Please hurry to the doctor's office. There's been an accident at the mine. There are a number of injuries and one man in very desperate condition, I'm afraid."

Her hand rose to her mouth while Fletcher spoke. When he finished, she said, "Tell the doctor I'll get dressed and be right in."

The doctor bent to Clyde, leaving those less wounded to the nurse. He felt it imperative that he give this last man his undivided attention immediately.

CHAPTER 18

Clyde's Dilemma

He gives power to the weak, And to those who have no might He increases strength.

Isaiah 40:29

Cutting away the last extracted miner's clothes, the doctor examined him for other injuries. He was badly bruised. Internal bleeding couldn't be ruled out yet. He cleaned the head injury and stitched the wound. Clyde's breathing had improved once some fairly potent pain medication was given to him. The doctor also gave him a tetanus shot.

Cutting away the man's right trouser leg revealed the ugly compound fracture. The tourniquet he'd placed on the left leg above the knee at the mine had stopped the bleeding. Still, this man had lost a lot of blood. He might need a transfusion. When the nurse got here, they would determine his blood type and look for a blood donor. More than likely, the poor fellow would lose the leg. They couldn't risk gangrene setting in.

Closer examination of the man's condition made the doctor certain that the best plan of action was to stabilize him here, and transport him to Doctor Showalter's Altamont Hospital above Hickok's Drug Store in Cambria. It would be difficult getting him up to the second floor hospital, but he was going to need surgery, most probably amputation. He hated to even think of that for such a young man, but that might be the only way to save his life.

A surgeon from Roanoke would need to be contacted immediately. From his perspective, they shouldn't wait any longer than necessary.

Walking out of his examining room, he found the young hero who pressed on to save this fellow. He was still waiting for news about his friend. He shook Fletcher's hand. "Young man, thanks to your persistence, he is alive. He has a tough road ahead of him. I can't tell you much more right now. As soon as that nurse of mine gets in here, we'll get these other fellows patched up and get someone to give you all a ride back home."

"I'm staying with him."

Clyde didn't have anyone else to be there for him. Rodger was back at camp recuperating. While Fletcher didn't want to risk losing his job, he felt his friend needed him more right now than the mine did. The doctor nodded.

It was past midnight when Clyde was transferred to the hospital. A surgeon came from Roanoke and surgery began around four in the morning. Fletcher managed to catch a nap on a hospital bench in the waiting area. He couldn't remember when he had ever been so tired. Physical exhaustion was one thing, but when you topped that with emotional stress, it took a toll. Running his hands through his hair, he suddenly realized how filthy he was. He found a bathroom and washed as well as he could. There was nothing he could do about his clothes, but at least his face and hands were clean.

He checked with a nurse to see if he could get a report about Clyde. "Excuse me, ma'am, I'm here with my friend. The fellow who was injured in the mine last night. Could you check and see if you have any news about him?"

"I'm sorry," she said, "but he is still in surgery. He has a very good doctor taking care of him. Don't worry."

"I'll check back in a little while, then. Don't want to be a bother. I'm just worried. Do you know where I can find a cup of coffee?"

She told him the drug store downstairs served some light food. Fletcher had noticed the place when he came in earlier this morning.

They were just opening up when he got there. He started to leave, but the two workers insisted he come on in with them. This was a regular occurrence for them. The counter girl started the coffee. She turned on the griddle to warm it up.

She turned to Fletcher. "By the time the coffee has perked, I'll be able to make you an egg sandwich if you'd like."

"That would be great," he said. "How much is it?"

"Ten cents. With the coffee, that'll be fifteen."

"That's okay."

About twenty minutes later, Fletcher was served his breakfast. He hoped he still had a job when he got back later today. He didn't have any way to get word to the foreman, but surely the other men would let him know where Fletcher was. He just hoped the growly man would understand. He thanked the girl for letting him in and paid his check. He bounded back up the stairs to check on Clyde.

He went by the nurses' station and she reported that his friend had just come out of surgery. "He is still unconscious, so you can't go back yet. The doctor should be out shortly. I told him you are here with him."

Fletcher went back to the hard bench and waited anxiously for the surgeon to appear. When he came through the doors, Fletcher tried to read his expression. The man looked tired, but there was something else, yes, hesitancy.

The doctor walked briskly across the hallway with his chart in his hand. "Good morning, young man. Fletcher is it?"

Fletcher shook the doctor's hand. "Please tell me, how's Clyde? Did the surgery go all right? Were you able to fix his leg?"

The doctor cleared his throat before answering. "Fletcher, I wish it was as simple as all that. This is going to be hard news to hear. We had to take his leg from the knee down. There was no saving it. He had lost too much blood and infection was setting in. It was the only way to save his life."

Fletcher sat down hard on the bench. He felt like someone had punched him in the stomach. "I…I don't understand," he said. "How will he manage? He doesn't have any family here to take care of him. He lost his leg?"

"Yes, he also had a pretty nasty head injury. We are going to be watching that. Your friend is still in a coma. We don't know if there is any further damage to his brain. There is some swelling, but it already seems to have gone down a little." The doctor ran a hand up his cheek. "Son, do you understand how lucky he is to be alive? I hear that he wouldn't have had a chance if you hadn't rescued him."

"Thank you," Fletcher said, "but I just did what any man in that situation would have done." He sighed. "I'm sure you did the best you could. I won't lie to you, I am upset about him losing his leg, but I understand. May I go back and see him for a moment?"

"Yes, the nurse will take you back. Please don't stay too long. We're not sure at this point if he will even be aware that you are in the room."

"Do you know how long he will be in here?"

"My guess is weeks. Sorry to be so vague, but we will have to take this day by day. He is by no means out of the woods yet. I'm just a surgeon. The other two doctors will be keeping an eye on him after I leave."

The doctor turned and left. The nurse let Fletcher see Clyde for a few minutes. She stayed with him. *He looks awful*, Fletcher thought. He went to Clyde's bedside and said a brief prayer for his friend's healing. He thanked the nurse and left the hospital.

What a fine young man, the nurse thought. She knew he'd received some tough news about his friend, but he hadn't lashed out like some people did.

When he finally arrived at the camp, everyone was anxious for news about Clyde's condition. Fletcher told them what he knew. He could tell from the men's expression that they were as shocked and distressed as he was. He asked one of the men about the others who had been trapped in the mine.

"They're all pretty banged up and sore. Mostly, they are just lying around today."

"Why are you all here and not at work?" Fletcher asked.

"They had to shut the mine down today. One of the bosses is coming in to investigate the accident. Everyone says it will be opened back up soon. They lose money everyday it's closed."

Fletcher put his head in his hands. He was so tired, but mostly he was worried about Clyde. How would he be able to support his family now? He couldn't work in the mine with just one leg, it would be too dangerous. Would he survive?

"Why don't you get some rest, Fletch? There's nothing more you can do right now."

"I think I'll do that," Fletcher said. "Let me know if you get any word about Clyde."

Fletcher entered the tent he shared with Rodger and Clyde. Rodger was out somewhere, probably over at the Henderson tent. Those little cat naps earlier that morning at the hospital helped, but Fletcher needed some serious rest. He fell asleep almost as soon as he lay down on his cot.

He woke up around three that afternoon. His body felt like someone had beaten him. He'd slept right through the midday meal so he headed by Mrs. Henderson's tent to see if she might have a biscuit or two left over. She was so glad to see him. She met him with a big hug and patted him on the back.

"I'm so proud of you, Fletcher Broce."

He felt his cheeks flush at her praise. "I didn't do anything special, Mrs. Henderson. We all just did what we had to last night."

"Don't be so modest," she said. "The other men told me they wanted to quit, thought it was useless. Thanks to you, the last three men got out alive."

"I guess you heard what happened to Clyde. I'm just sick over him losing his leg."

"That's not your fault, Fletcher. He is lucky to be alive, the way I hear it. I worry about all you boys everyday when you leave out of here."

"I heard you had gotten back to camp. Sit down, I saved you some lunch."

She served him up a plate of fried fish and boiled potatoes with a hunk of cornbread. Fletcher wolfed it down before thanking her and going on his way.

CHAPTER 19

Rachel's News

*Her children rise up and call her blessed; her husband also, and
he praises her:*

Proverbs 31:28

With everything that had happened since last night, Fletcher
hadn't had time to read Rachel's letters. He wished he'd taken them
with him when he headed to the mine. The letters might have been
lost when they were digging out the men, but it would've been nice
to have had them at the hospital.

Fletcher was determined to read both of her letters today. Lord,
he waited so long to get mail and then when it showed up, he couldn't
find time to read them.

He picked up the two letters and, using his pocket knife, made a
smooth cut along the top of the envelopes. The first letter was dated
November 12, 1919. Fletcher put the paper up to his nose and sniffed.
Was it his imagination or could he really smell Rachel's scent on the
paper? He was hungry for news from his family.

November 12, 1919

Dear Fletcher,

How are you, my sweet husband? The boys and I miss you so much. We've had a lovely time imagining what your long ship ride must've been like. We are not sure how much time it takes for you to reach America.

The boys are both thrilled that you've got to sail on a boat and ride a train. They can hardly wait to hear you tell them about your great adventure. We pray every night that you have arrived safely.

We are all hopeful that your job is going well. It cheers us to think that it won't be too long before we can join you. Do you have some idea of when that might be? It cannot be soon enough for us!

Now my dear, I have some exciting news to share with you. Do you recall that I wasn't feeling well when you left? There was a good reason it seems. I'm now almost three months along with our third child! Please don't worry; my sickness wasn't nearly as bad as it was with Arwood. I feel fine. I do tire easily, but I think that is because we have such energetic boys. They have been good, just boys, that's all. I don't know why, but I think this child will be a girl. What do you think of the name Dorothy?

Your parents and my Dad have been dears about checking on us and helping out when we need them.

We can't wait to see you my dear husband. I love you with all my
heart!

Love Always,

Rachel

Fletcher read the part over and over again about them expecting a baby. It never occurred to him that she might be with child. What must his family think of him for leaving Rachel and the boys at a time like that? God as his witness, he would've postponed his trip if he'd known.

After several minutes of berating himself, Fletcher felt a big grin turning up the corners of his lips. He was going to be a father again! Was Rachel right, would this child be a girl? That would be nice, a cute little girl who would look just like Rachel. He sat there on the wood stump, picturing his daughter.

Fletcher looked up and saw Rodger slowly making his way across the yard. He put Rachel's letters down and walked over to meet him.

"How are you?" he asked gingerly.

Rodger rolled his shoulder with a grimace. "I've been making the rounds visiting with some of the men who were trapped in that mine with me."

"How is everyone? I was so tired that when I got back I went straight to bed."

Rodger shrugged and winced. "About as well as can be expected. I heard about Clyde's leg. That's mostly what everyone is talking about. It was good of you to stay with him."

"I wish we could've reached him sooner. It could have saved his leg. He was still in a coma when I left. I guess he doesn't even know his leg's gone yet."

Rodger put a hand on Fletcher's shoulder. "I didn't come over here to get you down. I looked over and saw you with the biggest grin on your face. That's why I came by. Mail? From the little lady? Well, good for you. It's a good day for some good news."

Smiling, Fletcher said, "I'm going to be a father again, Rodger. Rachel didn't tell me before I left. Looks like the baby will be here next month. A girl, she hopes."

"That's great," Rodger said. "Good. Well. I'm going to let you be. I see you have another letter to read. I'm happy for you, Fletch."

After he left, Fletcher watched the sunset. That was something he and Rachel loved to do together. After dinner, she'd fix a cup of coffee for him and tea for herself, and they would sit on the back stoop, enjoying the sunset while the boys played. It wasn't unusual to find them holding hands and talking about their day while sitting there. He missed his wife. Missed her more than any time since arriving here in Blacksburg. Soon she would be here and they could continue their little traditions and make new memories together.

Fletcher read Rachel's second letter hungrily.

January 26, 1919

Dear Fletcher,

Greetings my wonderful husband. Hope you are settled in to your new home and job. Of course, it can't really be a home until we get to share it with you. Family is what makes a home.

Your family misses you very much, especially this past Christmas. We took out Mother's ornaments and as carefully as two little boys can manage – decorated our tree your brother brought and setup for us.

The children and I talked about memories with my Momma and Daddy decorating their tree when I was just a little girl. It's hard for them to imagine you and me ever being children like them.

Our new baby is growing and I have a huge abdomen to prove it. This is an active baby. I don't think it ever sleeps. The boys think it is such fun to feel the baby kicking, they just laugh and laugh. They are both predicting a boy, imagine that!

We can't wait to be able to mail our letters to you. Take care of yourself, my Love. We are keeping you in our prayers. Can't wait until we are all together again.

Love, Always,

Rachel

Fletcher placed the letters back in the envelopes. Words from Rachel and the boys made his heart want to sing. Today was Christmas for him. Hearing from his family was the greatest gift in the world. This was a tough life, but they were young and strong. As a husband and a father, he had learned that a hug and a kiss from someone you love could make any day better. He wished he had pictures of his family with him, but then again, it might make him miss them even more.

CHAPTER 20

Clyde's Homecoming

Fear not, for I am with you; Be not dismayed, for I am your God. I will strengthen you, Yes, I will help you, I will uphold you with My righteous right hand.

Isaiah 41:10

Fletcher made a number of trips back and forth from their camp to the hospital in Cambria to see his friend. Rodger accompanied him a couple of times, but couldn't stand to see his old friend in his present condition.

Clyde was staying awake a little longer now. The doctor was satisfied that there was no permanent brain damage. Mrs. Henderson and her husband had also paid him a visit. She cried at the sight. Her husband took her out of the room. Fletcher stayed and talked with him a little while.

But the words he had weren't good ones. "How could you let them take my leg? What am I going to do now?"

"You know I had nothing to do with that," Fletcher said quietly.

"I don't care," Clyde snapped. "You should have stopped them. What good am I to anyone now? I may as well be dead!"

The nurse heard the raised voices and came into the room. "I'm sorry," she said to Fletcher, "but you are going to need to leave. This patient needs his rest."

Fletcher looked down at his friend. Clyde wouldn't meet his eyes. "I'll try to come back later this week. Take care, man."

"Don't bother. It won't bring my leg back, will it? Will it?"

Fletcher bit his lips together and left. When he got to the hallway, Mrs. Henderson was trying to regain her composure. When she saw him she wiped tears from her cheeks and said, "Fletcher, son, don't take it so hard. He'll come to his senses."

"I hope you're right. I never dreamed he would think I was responsible for him losing his leg."

"He doesn't mean it," Mr. Henderson said. "He is just hurting right now and needs someone to blame. I'm sorry he is taking it out on you, of all people."

It was a quiet ride back to the camp. Fletcher knew his friend's feelings were unfounded, but it didn't make it any easier.

Two weeks later, Clyde was cleared for release. His leg would continue to heal and would require that the dressings be changed periodically. Mrs. Henderson was instructed by the nurse as to the proper procedure and was given pain medication to administer as needed. He was given a wheelchair and a pair of crutches and shown how to use them. He was an irritable patient and after days of his anger, Mr. Henderson began to lose patience with him.

"Enough is enough," he said one day. "I'm beginning to think what he really needs is a good swift kick in the seat of his pants."

Mrs. Henderson tried to shush his outcry. "For heaven's sake, man, would you hold down your voice? Do you want him to hear you?"

"I don't care if he does hear me," Mr. Henderson said. "It might do him some good. It's high time he started coping. I'm going over there."

Mrs. Henderson watched her husband trooping away towards Clyde's tent. The other men were at work in the mines. She worried that he would be harsh with Clyde. *Well, let him try to reason with him*, she thought. None of her well-meaning chats had helped.

Mr. Henderson entered Clyde's tent. "Hey, Clyde, let's get you loaded up in this here contraption and take a little walk."

Clyde looked surprised to see Mr. Henderson. He'd been laying there in the bed, like usual, just feeling sorry for himself. He agreed to go for a little spin with him.

Mr. Henderson liked that Clyde insisted on hoisting himself up and into the chair. He'd been prepared to have to do some heavy lifting if necessary. This would certainly make it easier on his back.

They moved toward the little creek at the back of the property. Mr. Henderson sat down on the grass beside Clyde.

"We need to have a little talk about your future," Mr. Henderson said.

Clyde laughed wildly. "That won't take long. I don't have one."

Mr. Henderson ignored that. "Have you written to your family about the accident? If not, you need to get that done. You don't want them to find out something like this from a neighbor. They need to hear it from you."

Clyde looked down at his hands. "No, I haven't told them. I guess I'm afraid they won't come. How am I going to get the money to get them here now?"

"I thought someone said the mining company was going to pay your medical expense and give you a hundred dollar severance? That's a lot of money, young man. You get busy writing that letter and I'll get it posted when I go to town tomorrow. Don't wait another minute. Let them know that you have some money coming from the accident and will be sending their passage when you get it."

Clyde swallowed and looked at the water bubbling along in the creek. But he said nothing. Mr. Henderson went on. Now, let's you and I talk about supporting your family."

"I'm a *cripple*," Clyde snarled. "What can I do? Sit around the house while my wife and kids have to work to take care of me?"

"You could do that," Mr. Henderson said slowly. "Or you could figure out what skills you have and how best to use them. You're not dead. You have something you need to work around, that's all. You're not going to feel like a man until you can contribute to your family's care."

"I don't want to be a burden on them," Clyde said. "But I don't see any way to avoid it."

"Clyde, tell me, what kind of trade did your family have in the old country?"

"My father and grandfather both worked making furniture. Repairing it."

"Did you learn the trade from them?"

He smiled bitterly. "They worked me like a slave. Yeah. I learned it."

"With the extra money you'll have left over, why don't you buy the tools and supplies you'll need? Start working on something. How about you start with benches? Your friends could use them in the tents."

"I don't know about all that. How would I get around?"

"I want you to think about something, Clyde. We have all these families coming over here with just the bare essentials that they can carry with them. They are going to need the things you already know how to make. They will need to either make the furniture or buy it when they get here."

"I see what you mean, Mr. Henderson."

"You're too young to give up on yourself. Let's get you going on a project. Mrs. Henderson and I have an anniversary coming up at the end of summer. Would that give you time to finish up say, one of those benches for her?"

Clyde nodded and palmed tears from his eyes. "Mr. Henderson, thank you. I know what you are doing, trying to set me up and help me get myself settled down again. Maybe you're right."

Peering out her tent door, Mrs. Henderson saw her husband and the young Clyde coming back toward the camp. She noticed something different on the young man's face. It looked like hope.

CHAPTER 21

Labor of Love

Then they journeyed from Bethel. And when there was but a little distance to go to Ephrath, Rachel labored in childbirth, and she had hard labor.

Genesis 35:16

A sudden, swift kick in her side reminded Rachel of the life growing inside her. Rubbing her protruding stomach, Rachel wondered about this new child. Boy or girl? Any day now, she knew she would have the answer. She already had a name for the answer she wanted. Dorothy. It meant "gift of God."

Men had no idea what women went through when it came to labor. But God was so merciful to allow women to forget the pain and remember the joy. The pain of labor quickly became a distant memory. She was reminded of a Bible verse, John 16:21: "A woman, when she is in labor, has sorrow because her hour has come; but as soon as she has given birth to the child, she no longer remembers the anguish, for joy that a human being has been born into the world."

She couldn't imagine going through this upcoming birth without Fletcher close by. With their other two children, Rachel felt like Fletcher's pacing outside the door set the rhythm for her labor pains. Had the Lord given her this child to occupy her mind so she wouldn't be so homesick for Fletcher? If she was totally honest with herself, she had been overwhelmed when she found that she was expecting again just as Fletcher was leaving them. It was daunting enough just being alone with two rowdy little boys to raise, a garden to tend, her housework, the cooking, the chores.

Rachel's body was letting her know her time was getting close. She had been having mild contractions and some familiar sensations like lower back pain. Something new this time around was her swollen feet and ankles. That meant keeping her feet up more, no easy task with two other children running around.

Her sister-in-law, Karen, had insisted on coming over to stay at her house this last week. Rachel protested, but now that Karen was here, she was enjoying the company and the help. It was nice not having to keep up all her household chores. Karen took over the cooking, the dishes, and the everyday care of the boys. She gave the children their baths and Rachel read them bedtime stories. They missed sitting in their Momma's lap, but her tummy was so huge, there wasn't room.

Fletcher's brother, Peter, came over and had supper with them each night. He enjoyed roughhousing with the boys. Joseph and Arwood loved all the attention. Uncle Peter got them so wound up that it took Rachel and Karen a while to get them calmed down after he left. He spent the night at his house, so his early morning hours wouldn't wake them, as well.

The next morning, when Rachel woke up, she was greeted with sharp labor pains. Karen noticed Rachel's discomfort and was concerned.

"It's okay," Rachel said. "Let's see how consistent these pains are. I would hate to get Mrs. Meyer over here too soon. Someone else might need her help more than I do."

Just as Rachel finished the sentence, the next labor pain rolled in. It wasn't long after the last. "Then again, maybe you'd better go after her," said Rachel. "Karen? I think you better take the boys to Hilda and John's house. See if Peter will go get Mrs. Meyer."

Another sharp contraction rolled in. Rachel felt a little panicked. It hadn't been this intense, this fast, with her first two children. She winced and looked up at Karen. "I think you better go right away. But will you come back here and stay with me until the midwife arrives?"

"I'll be back as soon as I can," Karen said. "I promise."

Rachel watched her wake the two sleeping children and grab their shoes. The boys looked sleepily at their momma, yawning and waving as they were whisked out the door.

Just as she heard them riding away in the wagon, another contraction almost took Rachel's breath away. She decided to imagine Fletcher there by her side. She was looking deep into his blue eyes and seeing his love for her and his family, it helped calm her nerves.

About a half hour later Rachel felt her water break. She was beginning to be afraid she might have this baby alone, but then she heard the front door open. It was Karen.

"Rachel? Peter's on his way to pick up Mrs. Meyer. Mama has the children. She was fixing breakfast for them when I left. She sends her love."

Rachel cried out in pain. Karen ran into the bedroom. "Rachel, what can I do?"

"My water broke right after you left," Rachel said. "The pains are getting closer together." Rachel bit her lip as another sharp contraction took hold. "You might have to deliver this child."

Karen blanched. After a moment, she said, "I've never done anything like that. I haven't even been around someone in labor."

"Don't worry. We will get through this together. Go get some towels from the wardrobe, just grab the whole stack and put them here on the end of the bed."

Karen rushed to the wardrobe and did exactly as Rachel instructed. She was a little older than Rachel, but had never had a baby herself.

Rachel had to wait for the next contraction to pass before she could speak. "Karen, go to the kitchen and put some water on to boil. Mrs. Meyer will need it when she gets here."

Grateful to get away for even a moment, Karen ran into the kitchen and put the water on. She stared out the window for any sign of Peter and the midwife. No luck. She was glad to be of help, but was still scared to death. She used the time away from Rachel to try to settle herself. She had to be calm. She prayed softly until she heard Rachel's loud moans from the other room. Karen hurried back to her side.

"Okay, now what should I do?"

Rachel squeezed her hand so hard it hurt Karen when the next contraction took hold. She didn't let go.

When the pain eased, Rachel looked at her. "You need to cut at least four strands of yarn into twelve inch strips. Use the white. After you get the yarn cut, get the sharp scissors off my desk and put them in the boiling water."

Karen rushed about to carry out the instructions. She cut the yarn and placed it by the towels on the bed. Back in the kitchen, she rinsed the wool fibers from the scissors, and then placed the scissors into the hot water with the handles upright. She certainly hoped Mrs. Meyer got here soon.

She went back to Rachel's bedside.

"Get a couple of those towels," Rachel said. "Leave them folded over and help me place them under my hips. There's going to be a lot of blood when the baby comes. Are you going to be alright?"

"Don't worry about me," Karen said. She hoped she sounded braver than she felt. "I'm not the one having a baby right now."

Another crashing contraction flooded over Rachel. She screamed out in anguish. "Help me lift my shoulders up," she breathed. "I need to push the baby out."

Karen placed her arms beneath Rachel and helped raise her up. Her gown was soaked with sweat.

Rachel screamed as she pushed with all her might. "Karen!" she screamed. "You need to help me. Pull the baby gently out when you can see its head."

Karen went to the foot of the bed. She could see the baby's small head crowned with dark wet hair. "Tell me what to do, Rachel."

"The next time I push, the…the head should come out. Deliver the should…the shoulders…*Oh my God, now!*"

Rachel screamed. Karen bit her lip so hard she tasted blood. She put her hands under the baby's head and her fingers on its tiny shoulders as it fell from Rachel's womb. It was slick with slimy skin and blood. "It's a girl," she said.

Rachel smiled. "Listen. Use one of the washcloths to wipe her face, then flick her feet to get her breathing started."

Karen followed her directions. When she flicked the baby girl's feet, the girl child screamed.

"Oh my God! Did I hurt her?"

The first cry of her new daughter sounded musical to Rachel. She leaned her head back against the pillow, smiling weakly. "No, Karen. She's fine. Now listen. I need you to lay the baby down easy and go get the scissors. Use a pot holder on them."

Karen ran to the kitchen and came back, holding the scissors out in front of her. They steamed in the air. Rachel nodded. "Good. Now you need to use that yarn. Tie the baby's cord in two places and then cut between the ties."

Karen's hands shook with fear, but she did just as Rachel told her. It was easier than she had expected. Disgusting, yes, but easy.

Rachel said, "Now look in that top dresser drawer and take out one of the little blankets. Just wrap her up in it and give her to me."

Karen did so. Rachel gazed for the first time on the sweet little face. It startled them both when they heard the front door open. In bustled Mrs. Meyer. "I see this little one couldn't wait for me to get here," she said. "What a pretty baby you have, Miss Rachel."

She turned to Karen. "You did well, young lady. What's your name?"

"Karen," she said. "What else do I need to know?"

Mrs. Meyer turned to Rachel. "You can nurse your baby now. And Karen? Since you want to know, the mother's first milk is the best milk for the baby. It will look a little different than breast milk, yellowish and watery, but it's filled with goodness the baby needs to be strong."

Little Dorothy latched hungrily onto Rachel's nipple and began to suckle. "Next," Mrs. Meyer said, "we need to deliver the afterbirth. Come up here, Karen. You can help with this part. Push right here. Feel that? That's her uterus. We need to massage it. Do that now."

Karen put her hands on Rachel. The midwife went to the kitchen and came back with clean washcloths and a mild soap. The baby was sleeping peacefully. She gave Dorothy her first bath while Karen retrieved a cloth diaper, pins, a little baby gown and clean cotton blankets. It was a joy to take her from Mrs. Meyer and gently dress her. She had Fletcher's startling blue eyes.

Karen wrapped the baby snuggly in a blanket like Mrs. Meyer showed her and carefully placed her in the bassinet. The little eye lashes fluttered a few times and she went right to sleep.

Next, they took care of Rachel's bath and put clean bedclothes on her bed. Rachel wanted to hold her baby some more, but the midwife told her she needed to have a light meal and get her rest. Karen went to the kitchen and warmed the vegetable soup they'd made the night before. She made Rachel some hot tea and put on a pot of coffee. Peter was out on the front porch. He had been worried to death about Karen, Rachel and the new baby.

She went out on the porch with him, but didn't realize what a sight she looked herself. She followed his eyes to her bloody dress and wet clothes from bathing the baby and Rachel.

"I'm sorry, Peter. I didn't realize what a mess I am."

"Are they both alright?" Her husband asked. He was bursting with pride that his wife had helped out.

"Oh yes. But I'm still relieved to have Mrs. Meyer here. Come into the kitchen and have a little soup."

Uncomfortably, he said, "Karen, Mama and the little boys are dying to get some news about Rachel, so I'm going to head back over there as soon as Mrs. Meyer is ready to go. I'll just sit out here."

Karen laughed gently at her big, strong husband. "Okay. I'll need to stay with Rachel for a couple more days. See if Mama will keep the boys over at her house. Maybe they can all visit for a little while tonight if Rachel is feeling up to it."

She went inside and took Rachel's lunch to her. Rachel fell asleep as soon as she finished her meal. Karen and Mrs. Meyer checked on the baby and then slipped quietly from the room.

CHAPTER 22

Camp Problems

The way of a guilty man is perverse; But as for the pure, his work is right.

Proverbs 21:8

Fletcher got up Saturday morning while Clyde and Rodger were still sleeping. Going outside, he found it was earlier than he thought. He couldn't sleep because he had Rachel on his mind. He'd never had such a compelling urge to connect with his wife. He felt like she and the boys were always on his mind, but while he couldn't describe it, this was different. It was as if he was sensing that she needed him right at that moment and here he was, an ocean away.

He decided to take a little walk to clear his head. May was a beautiful month here in Virginia. The grass was green, the trees were flowering and the mountains looked lush. He loved seeing them as they were now, with little wisps of fog or clouds hanging low and draped over them. This morning, the birds were just singing their hearts out. As he walked along, he saw does, fawns, rabbits, and squirrels. It would be a fine day for hunting, but he was thinking more about fishing later this morning with some of the men.

It occurred to him suddenly why Rachel was on his mind. The baby. It had to be close. Fletcher stopped and sent up a quick prayer for both her and this new child: "Lord, it's hard being so far away when my family needs me. Please watch over my wife and children. Be especially close to Rachel and this new baby. Please keep them safe and put people there to help her during her labor, I pray. Amen."

It sounded foolish, but Fletcher made a mental note of the date. May 24, 1920. Wouldn't it be something if this was his new child's birthday? Somehow he and Rachel seemed cosmically bound in this single moment in time. It seemed like a big stretch of the imagination, yet he couldn't shake the feeling that Rachel needed him at this very moment. Would they have a little girl like Rachel seemed to be hoping for, or another little boy? It didn't really matter to Fletcher, but if Rachel wanted a girl, he would pull for one.

He started walking back towards camp and noticed a wagon loaded with people coming down the rutted dirt road. *Another family moving in,* he thought. *Probably looking for work at the mines.*

The man threw up his hand at Fletcher. "Could you tell me where to find the Henderson's place? I was told to ask for them and they could tell us where to pitch our tent."

"You're in luck," Fletcher said. "I'm heading that way for breakfast. I'm Fletcher Broce."

The man sketched a little salute. "I'm Paul Conner. This is my wife, Helen, her sister, Anna-Leigh, and our two boys, James and Daniel."

"How are you, ladies?" Fletcher tipped his hat. "James, you and Daniel look about the age of my two children. Joseph and Arwood are five and three. How old are you boys?"

James spoke up, "I'm almost six and Daniel is four."

Fletcher couldn't help smiling. "Well, you fellows will all be good playmates with my boys when they get here."

"Where are they?" Daniel asked.

"They are still in Germany. They will be here with me in a few months."

Paul said, "Fletcher, jump up here with us and we'll give you a ride back to camp."

"Thank you, I'll do that."

As he hopped on board, he nodded at Anna-Leigh. She was a pretty young lady. He thought there were plenty of single fellows in their camp. They'd be setting their caps for her. He grinned, thinking about that.

Anna-Leigh gave him a flirtatious smile. She admired his muscular shoulders and trim waist as he sat on the back of the wagon with his long legs dangling over the edge. She bet he was plenty lonely with his wife so far away. Maybe she could stand in the gap and offer him her friendship. Who knew? Maybe his wife would decide not to come to America.

Anna-Leigh had, at first, not wanted to come here herself, but then their town started looking empty. She didn't want to be left behind to fend for herself. So far the trip had been incredibly boring. She questioned whether she'd made the right decision in coming. But, seeing Fletcher, she thought things were looking up. She was twenty-two. She and her sister had lost her father to the war years before and her mother died when Anna-Leigh was only fifteen.

For awhile, she'd lived with an elderly aunt. Her sister was a newlywed at the time. After a year or so, Paul and Helen insisted she come live with them. She was so grateful to get away from the old maid aunt who was so strict on her. That was about the time when her sister Helen had her first baby. Anna-Leigh wasn't much of a helper, but at least she was good company for her sister. She made it plain that she also wasn't a babysitter.

They arrived at the camp in no time. Fletcher jumped down and went inside the tent to find Mr. Henderson, who came out and welcomed the new family. He quickly pointed out a spot for their tent. "Come on back over after you finish and have a little breakfast with us. The Missus has been up since about five this morning getting breakfast ready."

Paul asked, "Are you sure you have enough to spare? We picked up some groceries on the way in, but we certainly are hungry."

"Oh sure, we'd be glad to have you join us. My wife cooks enough for an army every meal. Isn't that right, Fletcher?"

Fletcher smiled. "That's right, sir. Paul, some of us are going fishing about eleven, if you want to come. We do the fishing and eating, and the women do the cleaning and cooking. Works out pretty good that way."

"I do like to fish as much as the next fellow," Paul said, winking at Helen, "but my wife might skin me alive if I take off this morning and leave her with all the work to do."

The men chuckled. "I hear you," Fletcher admitted.

Fletcher and the guys had Mrs. Henderson pack their lunch. A group of them left promptly at eleven and headed down to their favorite fishing hole on the New River. They had plenty of earthworms to bait the fish with. It was a sunny day and fairly warm. There were a few high clouds, so they couldn't rule out the possibility of a spring shower. That wouldn't hurt a thing as far as Fletcher was concerned.

A couple of the younger men with them had already noticed the pretty Anna-Leigh. On the wagon trip down to the river, they quizzed Fletcher.

"Hey Fletcher, we saw you talking with that new family that just arrived. There were two women. Who are they?" a young man, Tucker, wanted to know.

Fletcher told them the family's names, but didn't elaborate. He was already focused on exactly what kind and how big that first fish was going to be.

But David, a young man a few years shy of Fletcher's age, wouldn't let him think about that. "So, that younger sister, Anna-Leigh, right? Is she married? How's she look up close?"

Fletcher laughed. "I'm sure the family is coming to the fish fry. Mrs. Henderson invited them at breakfast this morning. That is if you two can manage to help catch enough fish for everyone."

The men in the wagon laughed and teased Tucker and David about how the young lady would ever be able to choose between the two fine specimens they were. They took the ribbing good-naturedly.

They all enjoyed the peace and calm of being at the river. Fletcher looked across the river at the good land there. Someone, Fletcher couldn't remember who, had said that if you crossed to the other side of the river, it put you into another county. Pulaski. He wondered what that area was like. He wouldn't like the idea of having to get to and from work every day by water. It would be alright in fair weather, but winter would be another matter altogether.

By half past two, they had caught enough fish to feed both their crew and many more. Fletcher's mouth watered as he thought of the breaded and salted pan-fried fish. He hoped Mrs. Henderson would make some of her good cornbread to go with it. Maybe even some coleslaw, since the cabbage was already coming in at their community garden.

Mrs. Henderson was delighted to see the big catch. She got David and Tucker practically by the ears and enlisted them to help her clean the fish. She didn't get much protest from the guys. She was like a second mother to most of them. You just did what she told you to.

Fletcher walked over to Paul and Helen's tent to see if they needed any help and to remind them about the fish fry tonight. He announced himself and waited at the tent entry. They certainly were quiet. He hoped he wasn't interrupting the children's nap.

He had turned and was looking around when he heard Anna-Leigh's voice behind him.

"Fletcher! Good to see you again so soon."

He gave a polite smile. "Hello, Anna-Leigh. Hope I'm not disturbing you? I wanted to remind your family that we're having a fish fry at the Henderson's. It's later today. Probably around six."

Anna-Leigh thought he was probably one of the most handsome men she had ever seen. She loved his good manners and soft spoken voice. She touched his arm and let her hand linger there. "Thank you, Fletcher. Paul, Helen and the boys went for a walk down by the stream. Why don't you come in and sit and talk with me for a while?"

Fletcher felt his neck and face redden. He didn't want to be rude, but he was uncomfortable being around this girl. He certainly didn't think it was appropriate to visit with her alone.

"Thank you," he said, stepping back from her. "But I need to get back and see if I can help Mrs. Henderson."

Anna-Leigh laughed softly. *So he's shy*, she thought. *A challenge.*

Fletcher walked quickly across the yard. He might have misinterpreted Anna-Leigh's suggestive manner, but he didn't think so. David saw Fletcher walking towards him and narrowed his eyes.

"Fletch, I'm surprised at you. I know it's none of my business, but I thought since you were a married man, I didn't have to worry about any competition from you. Guess I was wrong about that."

Fletcher felt his blood boil. He turned abruptly and confronted the younger man. He shouted, "Now you listen. I have no interest whatsoever in that woman. And I don't appreciate your insinuations."

Mr. Henderson came up to them. "Everything alright here, fellows?" he asked.

"Just fine," said Fletcher. "Some people just need to mind their own business, is all." He turned and walked away.

Mr. Henderson looked at David. "You men usually get along good. What happened?"

David snorted. "If you ask me, I think our boy has his eyes on this new filly. And him a married man too!"

"I'm sure you're mistaken," Mr. Henderson said. "Don't let some woman come between you and Fletcher's friendship. I have never known Fletcher to be anything but honest and trustworthy. If he told you there's nothing going on, then that's the truth."

David stalked off towards his tent. He still looked steamed.

Mr. Henderson looked about. This was a tight knit little community. He knew others had probably witnessed that little scene playing out. He hoped this new girl was not going to create anymore disharmony. They didn't need it here.

He was proud of what good people they had living at the tent community. Family-oriented, every last one. He knew how much Fletcher talked about and was missing his own family. He'd heard him talking excitedly about how they would be arriving in the next few months. He didn't believe a word of David's take on the situation. Still, he'd watch and see how things progressed.

He'd hate to have to ask anyone to leave the camp, but they couldn't have a lot of conflict. These were hardworking honest men and families here. This girl sounded like trouble to him. But he would give her the benefit of the doubt.

That night, they sat up sawhorses and placed long sheets of plywood on them for a makeshift picnic table. The men pulled up whatever seat they could find, sometimes a barrel or bucket. Paul and his family came walking over to join them. He introduced his family and the others at the table introduced themselves. When David came over to meet Anna-Leigh, she looked right past him. She was scanning for Fletcher. She found him standing at the end talking with a couple of the other fellows he'd fished with earlier in the day. They were laughing and kidding each other.

"Excuse me--David, isn't it? I need to talk to Fletcher about something." Anna-Leigh said, before hurrying off in Fletcher's direction.

David was fuming. He followed her around to the end of the table.

She walked over and began gushing to Fletcher about how grateful she was that he had personally invited her to dinner.

The other men just lowered their heads in disbelief and backed away. *We're all homesick and missing our families*, Tucker thought, *but Fletcher is a married man. What's this all about?*

She tucked her arm in his and said, "I thought it was the least I could do is sit with you since you invited me."

David came up behind Fletcher and gave him a shove, nearly knocking him over. Anna-Leigh jumped out of the way. "What's the matter Fletcher? Isn't one woman enough for you? You got to make a play for all the ladies here?"

Fletcher had enough. He turned about to take a swing at him, but thought better of it. This was the part where he was supposed to turn the other cheek, right?

"Enjoy your dinner, everyone," said Fletcher. "I've just lost my appetite." He walked off in the direction of his tent. He heard someone behind him and turned to see Anna-Leigh running after him. He stopped. He couldn't believe this.

Anna-Leigh said, "Fletcher, I'm so sorry, are you okay?"

He held his palms out to her. "Stop right there. Let's you and I get something straight. I am a happily married man with a wife and children I love. If I have said or done anything that gave you the wrong impression, then I'm sorry. I think it is best that you just stay away from me."

He looked at the startled look on her face and thought, *Good, maybe I've gotten through to her.* "Now, if you will excuse me, I have a letter to write to my wife."

He walked away. Anna-Leigh clenched her hands into fists. How dare he treat her that way? Just telling her to go away? Other men were always more than happy to have her pay attention to them. This was not over. She would get him to like her, one way or the other. She put a smile on her face and headed back towards the table.

Mrs. Henderson came by Fletcher's tent about a half hour later with a plate of fish, fried potatoes, and cornbread. "Fletcher, are you in there?" she called out. "I brought you something to eat."

He invited her inside. "Thank you," he said. "You didn't have to do that. I'm sorry about all the ruckus earlier. Won't happen again."

"That young lady is trouble with a capital T," Mrs. Henderson said. "She doesn't seem to care much whether a fellow is married or not."

"I think I've made it plain to her that I'm not interested," Fletcher told her. "I don't know how this turned into such a mess. I'm not encouraging her in any way."

"Fletcher, honey, you will find girls like her don't need much encouragement. Now, that may not be fair to say, I don't know her at all, but I do know her type. I hope I'm wrong, but you just plan to give her a wide berth."

"That's exactly what I intend to do." Fletcher told her.

He thanked her again for bringing him some dinner. He promised to help clean up later.

CHAPTER 23

Making Plans

A man's steps are of the LORD; How then can a man understand his own way?

Proverbs 20:24

Rachel looked about their small home and delighted in the memories they all shared here. She had been a girl of seventeen when she agreed to be Fletcher's bride. It was hard to believe that she was now twenty-three years old and a mother of three children.

She couldn't wait to share this new child with him. Baby Dorothy's little brothers adored her. They always wanted to hold her. For about five minutes, anyway. Then, something else would distract them.

"Mommy, it's my turn to hold Dorothy, Arwood has been holding her forever," Joseph whined.

"No, I just got her," Arwood complained.

Dorothy was a good baby, and she was just a few weeks old. Rachel worried about the boys being too rough on her. She didn't want Dorothy to become involved in a tug of war with two older brothers. "I think Dorothy is getting tired," she said. "I need to feed her and put her down for a nap. Why don't you two get outside and play with the dog for a while? We have to take her to her new owners in a couple of days."

Arwood let Mommy take the baby. He and Joseph bounded out the door. The boys had been heartbroken when she told them their dog couldn't come with them to America. Rachel promised they would get another one once their family got their own house in Virginia. Some neighbors down the road had been thrilled to have the dog for their pet.

Rachel still tired easily, but she could feel her strength returning. She prepared them all a quick lunch from the leftovers from last night's supper. Hilda had made a pot roast and brought it by for them with a fresh loaf of bread. She called the boys inside, had them wash up and served them lunch. They surprised her by willingly going to their bedroom for a nap. Normally, it took a little persuasion. She certainly wasn't complaining.

When she covered them with a light blanket, she told them, "I love you two. Thank you for taking your nap so Mommy can try to rest a little too."

Joseph piped up, "Grandma is making us a batch of cookies this weekend if we behave for you this week."

"Have we been good?" Arwood asked.

Rachel gave them both a hug. "Yes, you've been real sweethearts, and I love you both so much."

Rachel stood at the door and watched the boys snuggle under the covers. Their eyelids were heavy and she knew they would be asleep in no time. She went into the living room, changed the baby, and nursed her. After burping Dorothy, she put her into the little bassinet for a nap. Now it was time for her own rest.

Rachel slept soundly for an hour or so. She awoke refreshed to a house of quiet snoring. She made herself a cup of tea and put her feet up for a minute. Rachel knew it sounded vain, but she hoped to get her figure back before she saw her husband in August. She didn't want him to think she'd let herself go while he was gone. She was pretty sure it was only natural to want to look good for your man.

Peter came by and brought her a fresh catch of fish he'd cleaned for them. "Karen is coming by before supper to fix these fish for you," he said. "So you'll have to put up with us for company tonight."

"Thanks Peter. You two have been so good to us. Do you mind mailing my letter to Fletcher? It tells him all about our new baby."

"Sure, I'll take care of it."

Peter walked over and looked wistfully at the sleeping infant. He and Karen always thought they would have a houseful of children, but that hadn't worked out.

"Does she ever cry? You are lucky to have such a good baby. Some of my friends have little rascals that just scream all the time."

"Not lucky," she corrected. "Blessed."

"I guess you're right," he said. "I've got to run. See you later, Rachel."

Rachel was relieved to get the letter mailed. It would probably be the last one she'd have time to send Fletcher before they sailed. His parents figured that they should arrive at New York City's Ellis Island by the middle of August. It was June now, but their time was quickly approaching when they would board the ship. She told him all about the excitement when little Dorothy had been born. The infant would be nearly three months old by the time they arrived and he finally got to hold her.

It was going to be a big transition for them all, leaving the familiar people, places and things behind and making their way in a strange new land. But at least Fletcher was already living there and would be able to help them all adjust.

She thought sadly about the possibility of leaving her own father, Amos, behind. He was a good grandfather and doted on her boys and the new baby. He said Dorothy reminded him of Katherine with her delicate features. The boys loved to hear Grandpa Amos talk about the horses he shoed and the farms he visited. They thought he had such an exciting job. They suggested to their mother that they needed a horse. Just a small one, of course.

She and her father still missed Katherine and talked of her often. Rachel regretted that her youngest son and the new baby wouldn't know their grandmother. Katherine would have loved them.

Amos seemed content staying in the little cottage where he had lived with her mother. She feared he worked too many hours now and didn't always eat right. He barely knew his way around a kitchen. When Rachel baked bread or made soup, she usually made a little extra and took it by to him. Maybe he would come have dinner with them tonight. He loved fried fish and his grandsons would be thrilled to have grandpa visit.

So far, there had been no question of him calling on some neighbor lady since her mother's death nearly three years ago. Warm tears drifted down Rachel's face. She didn't want her father to live a lonely life. She hoped he would find someone to love and take care of him.

Rachel tried on a number of occasions to have a conversation with her father about going with her to America. She knew he supported her and Fletcher's decision to go, but she wasn't sure she would ever be able to convince him to come with them. He told her he was getting older and had made many friends here. He thought at his age, America might be a nice place to visit. Rachel knew that he would never make that trip alone.

Of course, he wouldn't admit it, but Rachel suspected he was beginning to have some health issues. Amos was in his sixties. Sometimes, when he was playing with the boys, she noticed he got winded easily. He sometimes complained of chest pains, but told her it was just something he'd eaten. Rachel thought there was more to it and made a mental note to ask Doctor Smyth to give him a good check up. Maybe the doctor could try to make him take better care of himself.

Fletcher's parents were going to be closing on the sale of their farm next week. They would all be heading to the shore right after that. They planned to take the same merchant ship Fletcher had been on. The children were so excited. It was really special for them to get to sail on their daddy's ship. Fletcher had given his parents the name of the sea captain he worked for. He told them to let the captain know they were his family as the man had requested.

Plans were for Fletcher to meet them in lower Manhattan in New York City when they all got off the Ellis Island ferry. Thank goodness, Fletcher and her father-in-law, John, had ironed out all the details.

Rachel felt a little overwhelmed thinking of all the things she needed to wrap up at her house before they left. The same folks who were taking the dog were interested in most of her furniture and household items. Rachel wanted to get it all polished before they received it. That would give them a little more money to take with them.

The boys sorted through their books and toys and picked a couple of each to take with them. As a surprise for the children taking the dog, Rachel and the boys planned to hide their beloved toys and books they couldn't take in the dresser drawers.

Her plans were to pack just three bags, one with the clothes for her and the baby's items and a slightly larger one with a couple of blankets so she could tuck in family pictures and other precious mementos. Arwood and Joseph would carry the smaller bag which contained the boys' books, toys and a few outfits for each of them. It didn't sound like much, and the tough part would be deciding what to pack.

Rachel got on her feet and tried to go through a few of the boy's clothes and pack at least their bag today. She had contacted the lady they were purchasing the home from to let her know about their move. They were giving her the home back with all their improvements. She had talked with her father about moving into their home and taking over the payments, but he didn't need that much house or land to take care of. He had the ideal situation living right behind his employer.

She had half expected the communication with the seller of their house to be unpleasant, but to the contrary, she gave them her blessing and understanding.

It seemed everything was coming together beautifully. Rachel smiled and wiped a tear from her eye. She knew she was closing this chapter of their life, but had hope for what was to come.

CHAPTER 24

Wagon Loaded

I will instruct you and teach you in the way you should go; I will guide you with My eye.

Psalm 32:8

The sale of the Broce family farm in Germany went off without a hitch. They were fortunate to receive a tidy sum the day of the sale. It would go a long way towards purchasing a nice piece of land in the New River Valley. Their home was sold with all the furnishings, even the pots, pans and most of the dishes. There were a couple of bowls and a platter that had been handed down to John and Hilda that she couldn't bear to part with. Those were packed in their suitcases.

The departing wagon on its way to the shore contained a melancholy crew with their small collection of worldly possessions and wistful hearts. On one hand, the adults were resigned to the move, but each was leaving behind a little piece of their heart too. For John and Hilda, they were leaving friends they had known for a lifetime, the farm that had nurtured their family and a way of life. Rachel and Hilda both had borne all their children in their respective homes.

Rachel was saying goodbye to her father. He put on a brave front for them all, but his only child knew him too well to not see through his delicate charade.

The little boys were mostly going to miss their dog and some of their toys they left behind. That regret was more than offset by the excitement of getting to see their Dad.

Peter and Karen would not miss the home where they had discovered her inability to bear children. They remembered all too well the bitter tears of disappointment. Of all the people leaving that day, they had plenty of reason to look forward. Maybe in America, there would be medical advances that would help Karen carry a child successfully to term. They were a loving couple and had all the important people in their life traveling with them.

They made dusty tracks in the road as they watched the familiar surroundings slip out of sight. There was very little conversation as each seemed lost in their own reflections and daydreams.

In no time, the two younger family members were lulled to sleep by the clop of the horses' hooves. Joseph had leaned up against his Uncle Peter and Arwood's head was resting against his mother. Baby Dorothy--Dotty, they had all began calling her--was lying in Rachel's lap. Her bright blue eyes were alert and taking everything in.

The trip continued until almost dark. They arrived at a town that was about two hours from the shore, according to John. Everyone was tired and hungry. They stopped at a small guest house and had supper. They decided to spend the night there so Rachel and the children could get some rest. The men decided that they would get a room for the children and womenfolk to share. The two of men planned to sleep on the wagon. Hilda had brought along a couple of blankets. It was late June and very warm. They slept soundly under a bright starlit sky.

The ladies, while tired themselves, felt their mood lighten once they got all the children down for naps. They rarely had time alone with just the three of them to talk about their feelings about everything.

Karen looked at Rachel, who had a peaceful, content look on her face. "You're thinking about Fletcher again, aren't you?"

"Of course I am." Rachel admitted. "He's going to love this new little girl. And just wait until he sees how big his sons have gotten."

Hilda looked lovingly over at the new mother, "And, he is going to be happy to have his wife back by his side too. How are you feeling? It's still so soon for you to be traveling."

"Doctor Smyth said I should be fine, just to remember to get my rest so I don't get overly fatigued. I'm going to miss him. He was so good to my Momma before she died."

Karen came over and gave Rachel a hug. "Let me brush your hair. Sometimes when I've had a long day, Peter will brush my hair. It always helps me relax." She carefully removed the hairpins and using her fingers, worked out the soft tangles. She gently worked her fingers through Rachel's long locks.

"That feels wonderful, Karen. I'll have to get Peter to teach Fletcher that little trick."

Hilda may have just had sons, but she loved the two daughters the Lord had given her through marriage. "I don't know how the children and I would've made it without both of you helping us so much."

Each of the ladies prepared for bed. Rachel had put the boys on the floor on blankets, she and baby Dorothy slept in one of the twin sized beds while Hilda and Karen shared the other one. They all slept soundly. Tomorrow would find them boarding their ship to America.

The family was up early the next morning. There was an air of excitement today to displace the sadder mood of yesterday. Everyone was rested, fed and anxious to begin their new adventure. Change was not always easy, but by embracing the benefit on the other side, it could be uplifting.

Soon, they would reach the Port of Hamburg. One of John's friends told him his wagon ride would take him and his family to the

"Gateway to the World." John and Hilda couldn't wait to see their youngest son. Letters were good, but they couldn't replace being with your family. They were grateful that their home had sold and allowed them to reunite everyone with Fletcher that much sooner.

The women had heard talk of the huge fish market and looked forward to finding supper there later today. They had visions of open-faced cold, smoked fish sandwiches, such a delicacy! They might have to find the children some fried fish.

Joseph and Arwood were anxious to see all the ships. John and Hilda were going to try to find them both a little toy boat to take onboard to play with on the long journey. Rachel might scold them for spoiling the children, but they were worth being spoiled.

Karen relished holding little Dotty for much of the trip. The baby surprised them all by staying awake a good part of the day. This was definitely not the routine she was used to. Rachel couldn't ask for a calmer child.

Around half past two that afternoon, they reached the booming seaport city. Their eyes were wide as they took in the vast commercial wharf and all the activity here. They located their ship's dock and stowed their luggage in the area assigned to them. Peter and his Dad took the horses and wagon to a blacksmith shop and negotiated a fair price. In the world of supply and demand, the blacksmith did a steady business of this type due to the many emigrating families.

They caught up with the ladies and children on the sea wharf as they strolled along stretching their legs after the long ride. They all headed to the fish market to explore the many sales booths and to find their supper.

Peter and the two boys were walking ahead. Joseph and Arwood came running back to show their mom the brightly painted toys they found. One was a ferry boat and the other a steamship.

Rachel said, "How nice. I love the beautiful details; look at the little smoke stack on the ferry and the fat bottom on the steamship."

Both toys fit tidily into their small hands. Their eyes were imploring. Joseph begged, "Mommy, can we get them?"

"No dear, you boys take them back. We can't afford to buy toys."

"But Mommy," Arwood whined. "Please let us keep the boats."

"We have to watch our money. I'm so sorry, boys."

Peter helped the children find the vendor and return the ship and ferry boat. John and Hilda were walking behind the family holding hands. John winked at Hilda. Looks like the boys had helped Papa and Mama pick out the perfect souvenir for their grandchildren.

They reached the fish market and got the delicious smoked salmon sandwich atop a bed of lettuce and onion. The boys had some delicious fish stew with a little hunk of cheesy bread.

Soon it was time to head back towards their ship.

CHAPTER 25

Family Voyage

Preserve me, O God, for in You I put my trust.

Psalm 16:1

When the family arrived at the ship, they had to wait in a long line of boarding passengers. How could it be that they didn't recognize anyone standing there? John was beginning to realize how small his and Hilda's world was. They both grew up in the same little hamlet and attended the same school and church. Hilda made much better grades than him. He missed a lot of school because his Dad needed him and his brother to help out on their family farm.

After their marriage, he and Hilda made a pact that they would make sure their boys got an education. As fate would have it, both sons wanted to work on their papa's farm. They weren't interested in learning a trade. What a blessing his sons were to them both.

Rachel and Karen looked at all the people standing in line. Many were carrying heavy bags and as many as they could possibly carry. She was wondering if they should have tried to bring more. They had brought very little and trusted the Lord to provide for their needs.

She was hoping that Hilda had brought some pots and pans or they might really be in trouble.

Joseph and Arwood were so excited to get on the ship. They were both cooking up a scheme to take the ship by storm and run from stem to stern, top to bottom exploring to their heart's content. While they were waiting, Mama Hilda gave them the little toy ships they had picked out earlier with Peter. *When did they buy those toys?* Rachel wondered. She recalled John slipping away for a moment with Peter when they took the toys back to the stand. That must've been when Papa purchased the items.

When they reached the front of the line, they noticed the distinguished-looking older gentleman standing nearby smoking a pipe.

"That's got to be the captain that Fletcher mentioned," John said. "Let's introduce ourselves.

Captain Nelson was pleased to meet Fletcher's family. He told them that Fletcher was not only an excellent worker, but also a nice fellow. "When you see him, please give him my regards. And, if he needs a job, he knows where to find me. You did a good job raising that young man."

John and Hilda smiled with pride at his kind words. "This is Peter, our oldest son, and his wife, Karen. I don't know how we would've managed without him here helping us on the farm. And Karen's help, too, with Fletcher's wife and children."

The captain was somewhat surprised to see the tiny infant in Fletcher's wife's arms. He did the math in his head. Yes, the numbers worked out.

Joseph and Arwood were impressed with the captain's uniform and hat. He looked like a soldier to them. He promised to give them both a tour of the ship after they got to sea. With their mother's permission, of course.

Joseph assailed him with a barrage of questions. "Will you show us where our Daddy stayed? We want to see the kitchen too. Was our daddy a good cook?"

The captain laughed and tried to best explain Fletcher's job. "Well, I don't have to tell you what a big strong man your dad is. Mostly, he used all those muscles to help carry very heavy containers to the cook."

They moved on so as not to hold up the long line of travelers behind them. The captain thought about what an extraordinarily beautiful woman Fletcher's wife was. She was very quiet and preoccupied with keeping the children under control. She looked tired, yes, but beautiful still. If he had been a betting man, Captain Nelson would've wagered that Fletcher hadn't known his wife had been expecting a child before he had sailed.

After completing the registration and having all their names recorded in the big books, the family made their way down to the deck quarters assigned to them. The ship had cabins which were more expensive and limited in number. The lowest level of accommodations was called steerage. That was where they were bound to. They had been assigned four bunks. Their rooms were located near the ship's engine and a ship saloon of sorts. Their space was clear of debris, but had a slight smell. Rachel was glad she had brought the two blankets. She would put one on her and baby Dotty's bed and one on the boy's bunk. Because of a suspected cholera outbreak east of Hamburg, they all had to go to ship's surgeon to be checked for any infectious disease. They were given a clean bill of health.

Rachel's first negative impression was the lack of privacy. Each family was issued a chamber pot which they sat under the lower bunk and needed to be emptied each morning. And what about using the chamber pot? Rachel was picturing stormy seas and those chamber pots sliding across the floor and sloshing out.

How would they change clothes? Luckily that was not something they would be able to do very often anyway. She resolved not to worry herself to death over these things. Many people had come before her and would come after her. She would have to make the best of the situation.

Two hours later, they were full steam ahead. Peter and John took the boys topside to watch the ship launch. Hilda and Karen were taking a walk. Rachel was left alone to nurse the baby. She was more tired than she realized and so they took a nap together.

Rachel fell asleep easily, but slept fitfully. She had some crazy dreams and woke to hear Dotty's crying. She needed a diaper change. Rachel took care of her baby and held her close soothing her with a little song.

Everyone else came back with a bustle of noise and confusion. The boys talked excitedly about all they saw that night. They had met some other children, two boys who were their age with an older sister who was eight. They were going with their mother to some place called Pennsylvania to stay with their grandparents until their father found a job.

At last, Rachel got them settled into bed. She read Arwood's story book to them and promised Joseph she would read his tomorrow. Her sweet children went right to sleep. Peter and Karen talked for awhile about their impressions so far. Soon, they too became quiet as they settled into their bunks.

Rachel's stomach was feeling somewhat queasy. She thought it would pass shortly. When she went to bed, it didn't, the discomfort only got worse. The combination of engine oil smell, hot, stagnant air and the tossing about of the ship was more than she could take. She felt like she would be sick if she didn't get some fresh air soon.

She slipped from her bunk on the lower level. Rachel gently nudged Hilda to wake her.

She awoke and asked sleepily, "What is it? Are the children okay?"

Rachel nodded. "Yes. I feel sick at my stomach, that's all. I'm going topside for a minute to get some fresh air."

"Should I wake up Papa to go with you?"

"No, I'll be alright. I think I can find my way up there. Can I put Dotty in bed with you? I don't want her to roll off the bunk."

"Sure. You be careful, Rachel." Hilda took the sleeping infant and tucked her in between her and John. He barely stirred. It had been a long day and he needed his rest.

She looked at Rachel and thought she did appear a bit peaked. This trip may have been too soon for her after having the baby.

Rachel made her way shakily down the floor between all the bunks of sleeping passengers holding on occasionally as the ship rocked incessantly. She sincerely prayed she would reach the top before her stomach emptied itself.

CHAPTER 26

Nightmare at Sea

Give heed to the voice of my cry, My King and my God, For to You I will pray.

Psalm 5:2

As she climbed the last staircase, she felt the gentle breeze and the fresh air on her face. At last, Rachel felt like she could breathe. There was hardly anyone on deck, just a couple strolling further ahead and a few workers carrying items below. It had to be close to midnight, she thought.

While down below in steerage, she wondered whether a storm had cropped up. There wasn't a lot of starlight and she could see some cloud cover, but no rain. The big ship was chugging along, making steady progress.

She leaned out over the railing slightly, appreciating the soft breeze. She breathed in the fresh air, letting it fill her lungs. Her stomach seemed to be settling some. Maybe it was the fish she'd eaten earlier. But it didn't seem to bother anyone else.

She heard men's voices coming up the stairs behind her. They were loud and she thought sounded drunk because of the slurring and cursing. Rachel moved down the deck a little further hoping she was out of their sight. She would've had liked to have gone back to her sleeping quarters, but that would've meant going by those men. She continued to ease down the deck some more. She watched them emerge from the opening. They stood there awhile talking and laughing loudly, smacking each other on the back. Two of the men proceeded down the deck away from her. The other, a big, rough looking sort was coming her way.

Rachel had a bad feeling about this man, deep in her gut. She looked about to see if anyone else was on deck that she could go towards or call out to. She was probably being foolish, thinking those dark thoughts. She continued to walk away from the man. Maybe he would turn in somewhere and she would just go downstairs.

She found herself wishing she hadn't come up here alone. It was darker along this side, but she didn't know where else to go. She stopped at the railing and looked out to sea, hoping he would just pass her by.

The man came up behind her. "What do we have here?" he asked. "What are you doing all by yourself?"

"I'm with my family," Rachel said. "We just got separated."

"Looks like to me, you're lost."

"No, really I'm fine. Sorry to bother you."

He grabbed her hard on the arm and spun her to him. She could smell the alcohol on his breath. "Aren't you a pretty little thing," he said. "Now stand still. Let me get a good look at you."

"Please," she said. "I have to get back. My family will be looking for me."

He pulled her close to him and roughly squeezed her breast with the other hand. "I think you and me need a little time alone, don't you?"

He crushed his lips down on hers using his left hand to push her head toward him. He began groping at her. She couldn't get away from his grip. She prayed for someone to come along and rescue her. He heard a sound and turned to look. Rachel managed a weak scream. He hit her in the face and Rachel's world went dark.

The man dragged her behind some barrels on the deck and ripped open her blouse. The motion brought her back to her senses. "Stop," she cried, "stop, please stop--"

His hard punch knocked the breath out of her.

Hilda looked over at Rachel's empty cot. She got out of bed and pushed the blanket around the baby to keep her from falling and shook Peter, who was sleeping in the upper bunk. "Honey, get up. Rachel went upstairs, she wasn't feeling well, and I didn't like the idea of her going by herself. She didn't look good. She's been gone a while now, I must've dozed off. I need you to go check on her."

"Sure," Peter said. "Give me a minute." He slipped down from the upper bunk, inadvertently waking Karen.

"Is everything all right?" she asked.

"I don't know. Rachel's gone up on the deck. Mama's worried about her."

"Do you want me to come with you?"

"No, I'm sure everything's fine."

Peter put on his shoes and bounded up the steps two at a time. When he reached the deck, he heard a stifled scream and went running in that direction. He heard some strange sounds coming from behind a wall of barrels. And there he found Rachel.

Peter grabbed the man by the back of his shirt and jerked him away from her. He was a big man with big fists but Peter was beyond caring. In his black rage he beat the man's face over and over again. Blood gushed and the man shouted in pain.

The commotion attracted some of the other sailors. At first, they thought Peter was the aggressor and were trying to contain him.

One of them looked back and saw Rachel laying there practically unconscious. They sent for the captain and took the drunken man to the brig. He cursed and swore the entire way, trying to convince them that he was rescuing the young lady from Peter.

Peter took off his shirt and put it around Rachel. She was shaking and sobbing. The men helped get her down to the infirmary and sent for the doctor. Once they got her settled, Peter told her he was going to get his mother and Karen. Rachel cried pitifully, begging him not to leave her. He promised to be right back.

Peter went to the railing once he left the infirmary and threw up. What would he tell Fletcher? That his brother couldn't keep his family safe for even the first night of their trip?

The two women sat and hugged one another as they waited outside the infirmary for word about Rachel. The doctor carefully examined her and dressed her wounds. Rachel's face was badly swollen and bruised. He suspected she might have a cracked rib. He could tell it hadn't been long since she had given birth and was bleeding from the vicious assault. He couldn't tell how much damage had been done. He didn't want to tell such a young lady that it might affect her ability to conceive. He gave her a sedative to help her sleep.

He went into the hallway to talk to the three family members waiting there. "I won't sugarcoat this. It's about as brutal an attack as I've ever seen on a woman."

"Will she be alright?" Karen asked.

"She has extensive injuries. I have given her some medication to help her rest. How old is her baby?" the doctor asked.

"Not quite six weeks old." Karen said.

"It's going to take her a while to get back on her feet. Can your family help with the baby?"

Hilda sobbed, "She has three children. Of course, we will take care of them, they are our family too."

"The captain came by right after you left, Peter. He is giving her a private cabin to recover in for the remainder of the trip. He has never had anything like this happen on his watch and is greatly disturbed. Mrs. Broce, we all remember your son, Fletcher. I understand this is his wife."

Hilda nodded miserably.

"I don't want to move her tonight," the doctor said. "I'm going to let you come in and see her for a minute. She has been asking for you. But listen. She has been through a very rough ordeal, and she's feeling shame and guilt. What happened is not her fault, but me saying that doesn't erase her feelings. It might be good if one of you would stay here with her tonight so she doesn't wake up alone."

He put his hand on Hilda's shoulder. "I'm sorry this happened. Truly I am. We will do all we can to help her heal."

"Thank you," she said.

The doctor opened the door. "Rachel, your family is here to see you."

Rachel turned her back to them. Karen went to her and hugged her gently. "Honey, it's not your fault. You had no way of knowing." She gently rocked her like a baby as Rachel sobbed her heart out. "I'm staying with you tonight. Peter is going to be right outside the door. You are safe, sweetie."

Hilda hung back shocked at Rachel's appearance. She saw her pile of torn clothes on a chair in the corner of the room. She gathered them up, but didn't speak to Rachel. She looked at Peter and said, "Son, please take me back to our quarters. This is too much for me tonight."

Karen gave Peter a searching look. They would talk later once Rachel got to sleep. Neither of them would get much sleep that night.

CHAPTER 27

Setback

So shall the knowledge of wisdom be to your soul; If you have found it, there is a prospect, And your hope will not be cut off.

Proverbs 24:14

When Rachel woke up the next morning she hurt. The memories of last night's attack came crashing in on her. Her head was still reeling. Never in her life had a man struck her.

Rachel slowly sat up on the bed. She hurt all over. Karen was asleep in the chair by her bed. Bless her heart, Rachel thought, she said she would stay with me.

Rachel said her name. It woke her. "Are you all right, Rachel? Do I need to get the doctor?"

"No, but will you go get Dotty? I need to feed her this morning."

"I'll send Peter. I want to stay here with you."

"Karen, thank you for staying with me. I'm so ashamed because of what happened to me. How will I explain the way I look to my boys?"

"Peter and I talked about that last night when you were asleep. We think you should tell them you had an accident."

"Do you think they will believe that?" Rachel asked.

"Of course they will. You are their mother, they trust you. They are far too young to learn of such ugliness."

Rachel broke into tears. "Karen, what am I going to do? How will I ever tell Fletcher about this?"

"You will have to tell him the truth, Rachel. He can take it."

Karen stuck her head outside the door. Peter was wide awake and looked terrible with his black eye and bruised knuckles. He too, was sore this morning. Karen went over to him and gave him a hug. He was such a good man. She loved him with all her heart.

"Peter, I didn't get a chance to tell you last night, but I'm so proud of you saving Rachel from that terrible man."

"I just wish I could've gotten there sooner. It was the worst thing I've ever seen, him…him taking advantage of her." He took her hands in his bruised ones. "Karen, I have to tell you something. I would have killed him if those sailors hadn't showed up. I wanted to kill him."

Karen knew the emotional toll the night had taken on them all. "You saved her life," she said. "Will you please go get Dotty?"

He nodded but stayed for a moment longer. "How is she?"

"Alive, thanks to you," she said softly. "Go on, now. When you get back I'll find us something to eat."

When Peter got down to their quarters his family was just beginning to wake up. The two boys were sitting up in bed, playing with their toy ships.

"Hey Uncle Peter," Joseph said. "Where's Mommy?"

Peter looked at his mama and papa, hoping they would help him answer that question. Hilda looked away and John bowed his head.

Peter jumped up on the bunk between them and pulled them close to him. "Boys, I have to tell you some bad news and I want you both to be brave, okay?"

"What is it Uncle Peter?" asked Joseph.

"Is our Mommy alright?" asked Arwood.

Peter told them, "Last night, after you went to sleep, your Mommy wasn't feeling well. She had a tummy ache. So, she went up to the deck to get some fresh air. Remember, where we all went walking last night? She had a bad accident. She had to see the doctor and he has got her patched up now."

"Where is she, Uncle Peter?" Joseph asked. "I want to go see her."

"We're going to let her rest for awhile. I'll take you to see her later, how about that? I have to take the baby up to her now so she can feed her. How about if you boys go with Mama and Papa to get some breakfast while I do that? Aunt Karen and I will come get you a little later."

"Okay," Arwood said. The children went back to playing with their toys. Peter continued to hug them for a minute before he jumped down from the bunk.

"Mama, do you want to go with me to see Rachel this morning? You didn't get much chance to talk to her last night."

Hilda wouldn't meet his eyes. She changed the baby and handed her to Peter. "I don't have anything to say to her right now."

Peter looked at his dad for help. John just shook his head, saying, "Peter, we'll take care of the boys. Let us know if Rachel needs anything."

Peter didn't understand their reaction. More to the point, his mother's reaction. His father was just trying to keep the peace, he got that. He would try to talk with them later.

Taking Dotty in his arms, he looked at the sweet little face. He laid her head on his shoulder and cradled her little body as he carried her to her mother.

Rachel was glad to see her baby. Dotty began to whimper when she saw her mother.

Karen said, "Rachel, we are going to get breakfast for the three of us. We'll be right back."

When they left, Rachel looked down into the innocent little face of her child. She didn't think she would ever feel innocent or clean again. She felt so violated and mortally ashamed because of what had happened to her. She began to nurse her baby and cried her heart out the whole time. Dotty nursed until she got her stomach full, then she slept peacefully in her mother's arms.

There was a brisk knock at the door. "Ma'am, it's your doctor. May I come in?"

"Please give me just a minute," Rachel said as she buttoned up her gown and pulled the sheet over herself. Then she invited him in.

The doctor opened the door a bit. "Mrs. Broce, may I call you Rachel?"

"Yes, that is fine."

"The captain and his first mate are here with me. They want to speak to you about last night. Are you up for that?"

"I don't know," she said. "I'll try." She wished Mama or Karen was here with her, but maybe it would be easier if she did this by herself. It was embarrassing to talk to anyone about what had happened to her.

The three men entered the room. The captain came forward with his hat in his hands. "Ma'am, let me say how sorry I am. We've never had anything like this happen before. I hate this, but we need to get your testimony. May we ask you some questions?"

Rachel nodded. She didn't trust her voice.

The first mate said, softly, "Just tell us in your own words what happened last night."

Rachel's shoulders shook and she cried as she spoke. She explained that she passed out when the man struck her in the face and that many of her memories after that she saw as if in a fog. She remembered Peter pulling the man away from her and fighting with him.

The doctor looked at the captain and his first mate. "Gentlemen, do you have the information you need? I think this young lady has had enough for today."

They nodded.

Captain Nelson patted her shoulder gently. "Thank you Rachel, I know how hard it was to relive last night. You have been very helpful. Get some rest and let your doctor know if you recall anything else that might be helpful."

When they left the room, the captain felt like going down to the brig throwing the man over the side to drown in the sea. But that wasn't the law, as much as he wanted it to be. He would turn him over to authorities at the next port with a full report. He hoped he rotted in jail.

The doctor examined Rachel's wounds and talked with her to see how she was feeling. They planned to transfer her to her new cabin later that day. He had to be sure she was ready to be moved. He couldn't help with the scars to her heart and mind.

The doctor had just left when Peter and Karen got back. The coffee they brought was good. It hurt to eat because of her busted lip. She ate the grits and broke off little pieces of the toasted bread.

Peter told her about his conversation with the little boys. "They seemed to take it fine, Rachel. But seeing you might be another matter. Why don't we give it a day or two to give you time to recover?"

"We'll take care of them," Karen said. She smiled sadly. "It'll be good practice. You never know, someday, we might have a child of our own."

Karen's words hurt Peter's heart. He had long given up on the idea of them being parents, but Karen just didn't seem to be able to let it go.

Rachel nodded. "Will you ask Mama to help me get the boys settled in our room? When it's time?" She saw an odd look pass between the two of them. "What is it, Karen? What's going on with Mama?"

Peter said, softly, "Rachel, you will have to give her some time. This has all been very upsetting. I don't think she knows what to say to you."

"Is she ashamed of me? Does she think this is my fault?"

Karen's eyes watered and she hugged Rachel close to her. "Honey, I don't think she knows what to think. This is very complicated and she is grappling to understand it. We all are. Peter and I will talk with her. Don't worry about it. Focus on getting better."

Rachel nodded miserably. She could think of nothing to say.

The next week was a blur to Rachel. She moved to the cabin the captain had provided. She didn't want to leave the room because she felt safe there. It had a lock on the door.

After a few days, the boys came to see her. They were upset to see how hurt their Mommy looked. Rachel was relieved she had taken Karen and Peter's advice and given herself some time to heal before she let them see her. She missed them terribly during that time. At the end of the week, the boys moved into the cabin with their mother.

Hilda and John still hadn't been to see Rachel. It was almost as if Hilda was mad at her. She loved them and it hurt her that they weren't coming to see her. She just couldn't understand it.

John would come with Peter sometimes to get the boys and take them exploring on the ship with them. It was their men and boys adventure and the boys looked forward to spending time with them.

Today, Peter asked his father if he would mind taking the boys out by himself because he wanted to talk with his mother. John told him he didn't think that was a very good idea, but Peter insisted they needed to talk. Leaving the boys with their Papa, Peter headed downstairs for a much needed conversation with his mother. It might not change a thing, but at least he could say he tried.

He found his Mama sitting on a trunk reading her Bible. "Mama, we need to talk," he started.

"There's nothing to talk about," Hilda said. She didn't look up.

"I feel like you are blaming Rachel for what happened."

"She didn't have to go up there by herself. I tried to get her to let me wake up her Papa, but she said she would be fine. Look what happened."

"Are you blaming yourself?"

"Maybe. I just can't bear to look at her. Even if the attack isn't her fault, she's…she's *cheapened*, Peter. I can't help that I feel that way."

That was nonsense, and Peter knew it. "You can't forgive Rachel. Or yourself. And I'm betting you feel like you've let Fletcher down, too. I know I feel that way."

Tears started falling down his mother's cheeks. Peter put his arm around her. "Mother, there is no way any of us could have known something like that was going to happen, least of all Rachel. I know she misses you and doesn't understand why you haven't been to see her."

"I just don't know if I can do it, Peter."

"Rachel needs you," he said. "She hates herself for what happened. She's hurting. She did nothing wrong. She was just in the wrong place at the wrong time."

"All I can do is try," Hilda said. "I will. I can do that much." Her shoulders were shaking as she rocked and sobbed against her son.

"That's all I ask, Mama."

The next few weeks flew by for the family as the steamship made port in several towns along the way. Peter and his Papa watched at the first port as Rachel's attacker was taken out in shackles and turned over to the authorities. The captain and the first mate accompanied the police to the station to make their full written report and certify the charges.

"I hope they never let him out," John told Peter. "Ever."

Rachel was slowly getting her feet back under her after the vicious attack. It had been over a month now since that awful night. Hilda seemed to be welcoming. There had been no words of apology. She just started coming around again. It seemed that her way of coping was to pretend it never happened. She didn't want to talk about it, so Rachel learned to just keep her feelings inside around her mother-in-law. She didn't want to upset the delicate balance they had put back together.

Rachel woke up the next morning nauseated. She felt like her whole insides were going to heave forth. She managed to get to the chamber pot just in time. Her brow was sweaty from the exertion.

Oh God no, she thought. *Please no. Please.*

But in her heart, she knew she was.

Rachel climbed back into her bunk. She rocked back and forth, crying.

Joseph woke up, "What's the matter, Mommy? Why are you sad?"

Rachel did her best to compose herself. "I'm sorry I woke you up. Mommy doesn't feel well, that's all."

Joseph hugged her and gave her a kiss. "Do you want me to get Mama to bring you some medicine?"

"No, Joseph. I'll be okay. You lay back down for a while. It's very early."

A few days later, the ship's doctor confirmed her suspicions.

CHAPTER 28

Reunited at Last!

The spirit of a man is the lamp of the LORD, *Searching all the inner depths of his heart.*

Proverbs 20:27

From the time the steamship left the Hamburg seaport, Rachel had lost about fifteen pounds. Between seasickness, the trauma of the rape and now, morning sickness, she had no appetite. But she made herself eat when she could.

Karen was worried about Rachel's state of mind. She was depressed most of the time. She only smiled for her children. Her old sense of humor and joy of living was gone. Rachel had always been the most optimistic person she knew. She hated to see her like this. Karen knew Rachel was worrying about Fletcher's reaction. Would it be like his mother's first response? She certainly hoped not. She didn't think Rachel could take rejection from him. She wondered if she should break her promise and have Peter get to Fletcher first and gently break the news?

No, a promise was a promise. She and Peter would offer to watch the children so Fletcher and Rachel could have some time to themselves. Life didn't seem very fair right now, she thought.

They would make landfall tomorrow morning. Fletcher had explained to his father about the process at Ellis Island. Papa would help them all navigate once they got there. Karen didn't know what tomorrow would hold for Rachel. She prayed that the Lord would help Fletcher treat her tenderly and give him an understanding heart.

After dinner with the family this last night, Rachel and Karen, along with Peter and the boys, walked on the deck. It was a beautiful summer evening. Karen thought it would do Rachel good to get out with them.

She barely left her cabin except for meals with the family. They always heard the lock click in place once the men picked up the children for their usual outing. It was a sad sound that said Rachel didn't feel safe. Would she ever?

The men walked ahead a little. Karen was glad they did, so she and Rachel could talk. "Rachel, have you thought about what you will say to Fletcher when you see him tomorrow?"

Rachel's tears cruised down her face. They just seemed to show up all the time these days no matter how unwelcome. "Karen, I have had a hundred imaginary conversations with him. They all end the same way, with me in tears and unable to speak. What do I say? Fletcher, my trip was very eventful-- first I was raped and now I'm pregnant?"

She stopped at the railing. Peter looked back and gave Karen a questioning look. She waved him on and turned to Rachel. "Oh, honey. I think you underestimate your husband. I agree, the news will be shocking to him, but he loves you. Don't forget that part. He has loved you from the first time he saw you. I don't think anything is going to change that."

"I don't know what to think," Rachel said. "Karen, listen. I think about the joy I've felt, carrying my babies. With this one, I feel nothing but anger. And God help me, even hate."

"I think that's fair," Karen said. "It's normal. Look. Peter and I've talked. When we get ashore, we will take the boys exploring. That will give you time alone with Fletcher."

Rachel looked down. "I used to have such happy dreams about seeing Fletcher again. Now all I feel is dread. Why did that man have to spoil everything for us?"

"Don't give him that power," Karen said. "Take it back. You've got your whole life ahead of you."

Rachel palmed away her tears. "Karen, I love you. I couldn't have gone through any of this without you and Peter, but I'm not brave like you."

"You arc stronger than you think, girl."

The next day, right on schedule, they dropped anchor outside of Ellis Island. They took the ferry ashore. It was a hot sunny day. Peter held onto Joseph and Arwood. They all stared at the massive Statute of Liberty. John and Hilda thought she was beautiful. Peter and Karen kissed and the little boys thought that was disgusting. Peter turned around and tickled them and they both erupted in a fit of giggles.

Rachel hung back. Her mind was racing and she thought she might get sick. She looked around at all the happy faces and wished she could share their glee. This should be a happy occasion, but she was still filled with apprehension. Or was it just plain fear?

When the family disembarked at the island, Rachel felt swept up into the crowd of people. They were efficiently shuttled through the snaking lines. Looking about at all the people assembled there, Rachel thought she witnessed every possible emotion. She looked at her children. Their eyes sparkled as they laughed and played with each other. They were her life. She needed to get back to that happy place again, but how? She still felt so lost.

All too soon they boarded the ferry and headed for lower Manhattan. Rachel's eyes searched the waiting crowds at the ferry dock when they arrived. At first, she didn't see Fletcher, and then there he was, right up front. She had to smile, how could she miss him? She had almost forgotten how handsome he was. He was jumping up and down and shouting enthusiastically. He had spotted all of them right away.

His eyes met Rachel's and locked. There she was. He had missed her with every fiber of his being. He searched her face; it looked like she had been crying. Oh well, more of those tears of joy. Women! He saw the small, sleeping bundle in her arms, his first daughter. He couldn't wait to see and hold her. His eyes scanned the faces of his family. There was Mama, Papa, the boys, Peter and Karen. They were all waving frantically at him.

This is what life is all about, he thought. *Family.*

Fletcher gently pushed forward towards them. He took Rachel in his arms and kissed her as if he needed to drink her in. He didn't remember her being so thin. He looked at the face of his sleeping daughter and felt her little fingers lock around his.

Joseph and Arwood were jumping on him vying for his attention. Fletcher looked down and scooped the two boys up. He couldn't believe how big they'd gotten. Arwood was just a toddler when he left and look at him now, he was a little boy. Joseph was so handsome with his thick hair. They showed him their new toy boats Mama and Papa had bought them. Some things never changed. Mama and Papa were still spoiling his boys.

He hugged his mother and kissed her tearful cheek. He and his father hugged. John looked like he had lost some weight too. Fletcher knew he had worked hard at the farm keeping them all fed. Just him and Peter with all that work, when it was at least a three-man job.

Fletcher grinned at his big brother and gave his wife, Karen, a hug around the shoulders. "Thanks for taking care of them for me, Peter. I don't know how I will ever repay you."

Peter's face darkened for just a moment. Fletcher studied his brother. Peter's old smile returned, but Fletcher knew he had seen something there. He wondered if he and Karen were having problems. Karen looked a little guarded too, now that he took a second look. They would have time to talk later.

Fletcher took Rachel's bags and led his family away from the docks.

CHAPTER 29

Big Decisions

A good name is to be chosen rather than great riches, Loving favor rather than silver and gold.

Proverbs 22:1

As they approached the city, Fletcher explained that he had secured two rooms for them for the night. Mama, Papa, Peter and Karen would stay in one, he and his family in the other.

"Son," John said, "thank you. But your mother and I will pay for our room."

"Later," Fletcher said. "But the first night's on me." He smiled ruefully. "That's all I could afford. Your room is on the first floor. Rachel's and mine are upstairs."

They were within walking distance of the house. It felt good to set their bags down and get off their feet for awhile. Peter told Fletcher that he and Karen wanted to take the boys out exploring the city that afternoon.

Fletcher told him, "There is a big park right here in the city. It has lots of trees, a huge pond and sheep in the meadow. There are street vendors, so you may be able to get a sandwich there." Fletcher offered him a dollar. "Here. For some food."

"This is our treat," Peter said. "We'll wash up and head out. Why don't you and Rachel take advantage of this time alone and go out to dinner somewhere nice?"

Fletcher put the money back in his wallet. "Okay. I arranged for someone to take pictures of our family tonight. A surprise for Rachel. Let's try to get Mama and Papa to get theirs taken, too."

"I like that," Peter said.

"Be back here by seven, okay? The photographer will be here. He wants to take the picture on the steps of the house we're staying at."

Peter hoped the evening would work out for him and Rachel. He silently prayed for peace and understanding for the couple once Rachel broke the news to him.

Rachel had been so quiet. Fletcher thought she was just tired. He remembered how tired he was when he got through the ordeal at Ellis Island. Poor Rachel had all the children to get processed too. He was so glad the rest of the family was able to travel with her.

When he got to the room, Rachel had fed baby Dotty and put her down for a nap. She'd freshened up herself, put on a clean blouse and combed her hair. She was acting a bit shy around him, but he chalked it up to their time apart.

He took her in his arms and kissed her gently. "I love you," he said. He wanted to hold her in his arms forever. How right it felt having his arms around her. "You are more beautiful than ever to me. I have missed you so much."

He tilted her chin up towards him so he could look into her beautiful eyes. He swore he saw pain there.

"Rachel? Are you okay?"

"I have something I need to talk with you about," she said. "But it can wait."

"What is it, Rachel? We've always been able to talk about everything, haven't we?"

She bit her lip and looked away. After a long moment, she told him.

He sank into the chair by their bed. "I should never have let you come by yourself," he said, his voice breaking. "I should've been with you to keep you safe. This is all my fault."

Rachel looked down at her feet. "Fletcher. I…I'll understand if you don't want me now. I will."

Standing, he took her in his arms again and squeezed her close to himself. "You're not to blame. I will never stop wanting you and loving you. I'm just sick about what happened to you. I don't know how you've gotten through this on your own."

She started to cry. "I haven't done so well. I don't know what I would've done if it hadn't been for Peter and Karen helping with the boys. I still cry myself to sleep every night."

Fletcher held her as she cried into his shoulder. After a time she took his hands in hers and found the courage to tell him the rest. "I'm pregnant."

"Are…are you sure? Have you seen a doctor?"

"Yes. The ship's doctor. He confirmed it. I don't expect you to want me now. I understand if you don't."

"Rachel, I…I don't know what to say. How could this be happening to us?"

She hated the pain her words had inflicted on him. But they had needed to be said. "I know, Fletcher. I've asked myself that same question at least a thousand times."

"What are we going to do? You have to get rid of this baby!"

Rachel burst into fresh tears. "I know I can't love this child. But I cannot destroy a life either."

"Rachel, that baby will destroy *our* life. What will people in Virginia say when you show up pregnant? They'll think you are nothing but trash. I won't have anyone think of you that way."

"I know," she said miserably. "Do you want to divorce me?"

"Oh my God, no, Rachel. I would die without you in my life. But, I'm lost here. I don't have any answers. Does Mama, Papa and everyone else know about this?"

"Mama and Papa know about the…the rape, but they don't know about the pregnancy. I told Karen. I had to have someone to talk to. I asked her not to tell them. But I'm sure she probably told Peter."

"Let's keep it that way for now. There is no reason to get Mama and Papa involved in this whole ugly mess." Fletcher said. "Let's take a walk. We can talk some more. I suddenly feel suffocated in this room."

They gathered the sleeping baby and slipped out the door.

Rachel and Fletcher walked along. They stopped at a café and shared a sandwich and ordered iced tea. It was very refreshing on the hot August night.

Baby Dotty woke up and Fletcher looked into those brilliant blue eyes. It was like looking into the mirror. She had his eyes, but looked just like her mother. She gave him the sweetest little toothless smile.

"She is the best baby, Fletcher. Her little brothers love her to pieces."

"Rachel, I see you when I look at her. She'll break hearts someday."

"I've broken your heart," Rachel said. "Haven't I?"

"I won't lie to you. I feel like I'm living out a very bad dream right now. I don't know why you'd want to keep that baby."

"Fletcher, I would feel like a murderer if I killed it."

"Is it really even a baby yet? Does its heart beat when it's so young?"

"Fletcher, I don't know the answer to those questions. I just know that I've always thought of a baby as a gift from God."

"How could this be from God? Why would He punish us like this? I don't understand."

"I don't understand it either, but I don't think God would have put this child in our path to destroy it." She reached across the table and took his hands. "I thought of something, but you may think this is crazy. What if I have this child and give it Peter and Karen? That's how this baby could be a gift, too."

"I don't know, Rachel. How could we do that?"

"We could tell Mama and Papa that Karen is going to have a child that we are worried about her traveling to Virginia in her delicate state. I could say I was staying with her to take care of her while you and the boys and your parents go back to Virginia and work on a home for us all."

He thought about it for a long time. Finally he said, "It might work. But, then I have to be away from you for almost a year again. How will the boys ever manage without you?"

"They will have you and their Mama and Papa. The real question is, how will I manage without them and you?"

Rachel looked at her husband. She loved him so much. She couldn't imagine living her life without him. For the first time since that horrible first night on the ship, she felt hopeful.

"Let's talk to Peter and Karen and see what they think of your idea, Rachel."

"Karen wants a baby so bad, I'm hoping they will see this child as a gift and love it unconditionally."

"I honestly don't know what their reaction will be, Rachel. We'll talk with them after they get back with the boys."

Fletcher and Rachel walked back to the house where they were spending the night. Nothing was the way they thought it would be for their reunion. He told her about the photographer. When Peter and Karen showed up, they had just enough time to get the boys ready. A very important conversation would have to wait.

CHAPTER 30

Grace Abounds

"Many daughters have done well, But you excel them all."

Proverbs 31:29

The session went well. Mama and Papa had their picture taken together, Peter and Karen, Fletcher and Rachel, the three children, Fletcher with Rachel and the three children, the entire family, and one of each person individually. The shutter clicking sounded like a cash register to the eager photographer.

The hardest part for the children was not smiling. The photographer wanted all of them, including the children to have a serious expression on their face. He said it made for a better picture. It wasn't hard for the rest of the family to present a somber mood. The adults all knew Fletcher had heard the news for the first time. They could see the pain on his handsome young face and Rachel's tear-streaked cheeks.

Everyone settled up with the photographer. He told them the pictures would be placed in the mail to them in three weeks.

Mama and Papa retired to their room. Papa raised the window some to let in a little air before he went to sleep. Peter and Karen decided to take a short walk around the neighborhood.

Fletcher and Rachel got the children inside and ready for bed. Rachel had to feed Dotty and get her down for the night. It was a treat for the boys to have Daddy read their bedtime story tonight. Before he read their book, he had a little wrestling match with them. They both jumped on him at once, all giggles, legs and arms.

Rachel had to smile watching them. Even with everything that had happened, she had to smile. He finally got them settled down for bed and gave them both a hug.

Joseph said, "I love you Daddy. I didn't think we would ever see you again."

"Ah, Son, I told you we'd be together soon. Didn't you believe me?"

"I know, you were gone a long time and Mommy has been sad."

"You know what, Joseph? I have been sad without all of you too."

He gave him a hug and covered the sleeping Arwood, kissing his forehead.

Once they were sure the children were all asleep, they slipped downstairs to meet Peter and Karen on the front steps.

Fletcher asked them to meet them out there in about an hour. Peter thought he just wanted to catch up and quickly agreed. It would be good to talk to his little brother. They had all missed him, but were very proud of him too.

The evening was still warm, but there was a nice gentle breeze making it bearable. Peter had talked the owner of the house into putting on a pot of coffee. His persuasion and a nice tip had done the trick.

The four of them settled down on the broad steps of the boarding house. Fletcher looked over at Peter. "I want to thank both of you for helping Rachel with the children while I've been gone."

"We have loved spending more time with the children," Karen said. "They are very special to us." And then, almost as an afterthought, "To both of you, too. Of course, I never expected to be delivering your daughter. I was scared to death. I was never so glad to see anyone as I was that midwife."

They all laughed. "And Peter was a big help once he got there," Karen said, smiling. "I couldn't even get him to come in the house till all the excitement was over."

"If I'd been home, I would've been out there on the porch with you, Peter. You remember, Rachel tried to bite me when Arwood was born?"

"Why do you think I stayed on the porch?"

They sipped their coffee and enjoyed the nice evening and the company. After a time, Fletcher said, "Peter, this is hard to talk about, but I need to say this. Thank you for coming to Rachel's rescue when that monster attacked her."

Peter looked down at his hands. But he said nothing.

Rachel said, "And I couldn't have survived that awful night without you, Karen."

Fletcher looked at the two of them, "Rachel tells me that you both know about our little problem."

Peter nodded slowly. "Yes. Karen told me. We made sure Mama and Papa didn't know anything about it, though." He looked at his brother. "I'm sorry, Fletcher. What are you and Rachel going to do? About the baby, I mean?"

Fletcher searched their faces. They were such a sweet couple, always had been. It was too bad they'd never had children, they would make great parents. His children loved them dearly.

"That's part of what we want to talk with you both about. I'll tell you honestly, I want Rachel to get rid of the baby. I've heard there are some less-scrupulous doctors who will help with this kind of problem."

Karen said, "No one can blame you for thinking that way, Fletcher. Rachel and I have talked about that too. We both think it's a sin to take the child's life, but only the two of you can decide what's right for your family."

"I agree with Rachel that the baby is an innocent and shouldn't have to die to pay for its father's crime. The problem is that we don't have much time to make a decision. I don't want Rachel to come to Virginia and have this baby, if that's what she has to do. Everyone would talk about her and our family."

Rachel spoke up. "I thought I could stay here and have the baby, then put it up for adoption. I know I can't love this child the way I do our own. It wouldn't be fair to the baby."

Fletcher said, "I don't want Rachel to stay here alone. Would you two be willing to stay with her? I can send whatever money I can spare to help out."

"What would you tell everyone in Virginia about why Rachel didn't return with you?" asked Karen.

"We don't have that figured out yet," said Fletcher.

"Karen, what do you think? Are you willing to have us stay with Rachel? I can probably pick up some work here."

Karen took Rachel's hand. "Yes. We'll do anything to help."

"Thank you," Rachel whispered.

Karen looked at her husband. He looked at her for a long time. She nodded and after a moment, he smiled. "Let's make it ours," he said. "Can we?"

Karen hugged her husband's neck. Tears were streaming down her face when she answered him. "Yes Peter. We can. What will we tell Mama and Papa?"

Peter said, "Why, we'll tell them we are expecting and that Rachel is staying here to help you with the baby."

Karen laughed, "Well, that certainly is true."

Peter and Karen went into their room as quietly as possible so as not to wake the older couple. Peter was surprised to see his mother standing by the window. He noticed the curtain rustling gently in the evening breeze. How much had she heard? Had she heard anything at all?

No one asked. It was better that way.

CHAPTER 31

New Beginnings

She girds herself with strength, And strengthens her arms.

Proverbs 31:17

Everyone in Peter and Karen's room woke up bright and early the next morning and refreshed from the good night's rest in a real bed. Peter and Karen were the first ones out of the room. They snagged a cup of coffee and sat on the porch watching the sunrise together.

Peter looked at the soft sunlight on Karen's face. Her blonde hair looked like gold. She looked radiant with a peaceful smile on her face. He leaned over and kissed her.

"You look happy this morning," he said.

"Oh Peter, I am. It's all going to work out, isn't it?"

"It is," he said.

"She didn't deserve what happened to her."

"No," he said. "She didn't. But this is making the best of it. I'm not sure how they want to explain this to Mama and Papa. Or how we want to."

"We need a little privacy with Rachel and Fletcher to talk about our story."

"Our story. I like that."

"No regrets, Peter?

"None whatsoever."

Fletcher woke to the sound of two little boys softly snoring and the baby making her little sounds. He could get used to this. Absolutely. He picked up baby Dotty and was instantly rewarded with one of the cutest smiles. He walked over to the window and looked out at the sunrise. This was a new day. He was glad yesterday was behind them all. He was surprised to see Peter and Karen sitting out there on the front steps this morning. They looked so peaceful and in love.

He couldn't believe that they were willing to step up for him and Rachel the way they did. It couldn't be easy for them. He hoped this baby would be as much a blessing for them and they were to him and Rachel.

Rachel opened her eyes and was pleasantly surprised to see her sweet husband already up and playing with the baby. Dotty was studying her Daddy and grinning at him. She was trying her best to talk to him with all her little baby sounds.

Rachel got out of bed and went over to put her arms around both of them. He smiled up at her and said, "I love you Mrs. Broce." He kissed her soft lips.

"I love you too, Mr. Broce," she said, smiling.

"Look out the window. Peter and Karen are sitting out there on the steps. They look like they haven't a care in the world."

"I can't believe they have agreed to our plan. I hope this baby will be a source of great happiness to them."

"To two as thirsty as they are for a family, the baby will be as welcome as water. I don't say that to take away from what a grace-filled thing they're doing for us."

"I love the way you put that. I feel like I can breathe again."

He put his hand on her leg and rubbed circles with his thumb. She smiled at him. "I wish you didn't have to leave today."

"I'm afraid to stay too long. The mine foreman can be a grudging fellow. I wouldn't want to risk losing my job. I'm lucky I was able to come up here. It is without pay, of course."

The boys woke up and shrieked in excitement at the sight of their daddy. He handed Dotty off to Rachel and grabbed Joseph and Arwood, and spun them around. They laughed and played while Rachel fed the baby. She smiled watching them all together. It wouldn't be long before they could be reunited on a more permanent basis.

Fletcher told them Uncle Peter and Aunt Karen were outside on the porch. Off they scampered barefoot to see them. He wanted to get them out the door, so he and Rachel could talk out how they would communicate their plan to his parents. That was going to be the hard part. His Mama was pretty astute and always seemed to see right through them all.

Rachel hated the deception, but agreed with Fletcher that it was necessary. She prayed the next seven to eight months would go by fast.

She and Fletcher sat by the window and held each other. They could hear the children's laughter. Peter was so good with his little nephews. He would make a good father.

"Rachel, I'm going downstairs and talk with Peter and Karen. I'll send the boys back up to you. Hopefully, Mama and Papa won't come outside right now. You and I will catch up when I get back."

Fletcher shooed the boys back upstairs with their Mommy so she could get them ready for breakfast.

"It won't hurt you to comb that hair," he called after them. They were such happy children. He dreaded telling them their Mommy was staying up here with two of their favorite people, Uncle Peter and Aunt Karen.

Karen said, "I think I'll go help Rachel with the children this morning. Mama and Papa are up. Why don't you take a walk and sort all this out?"

Peter smiled gratefully. He wanted some time alone with his brother. They hopped to their feet and headed down the street.

"Fletcher, you know what? I'm proud of you, little brother. A lesser man couldn't take all the bad news, hurt and disappointment that was sprung on you yesterday. I know it hasn't been easy, but you took it like a man."

"You're right about that 'not easy' part. I feel like my heart was torn out of me. I can't think too much about what happened to Rachel on that ship without wanting to kill that man."

"Papa and I felt the same way. I think that's only natural. But that's the difference, we think about it in our anger, but we don't act on it. People like that crude fellow have no impulse control."

"I wish there was some way to know what his punishment will be."

"Fletcher, let it go. The evidence and testimony the captain and first mate gathered should ensure he doesn't bother any other woman for a good long while."

"Peter, I can't tell you how much it means to Rachel and me to have you and Karen help us out like you are."

"The way I see it, little brother, you and Rachel are helping us. Karen is so excited about this baby. We do see the child as a gift from God."

"I can't believe I've waited all this time to have Rachel and the children here with me and now, we'll be separated again."

"That time will fly by, brother. The women have figured that the baby will be here near the end of March. We will travel your way as soon as Rachel is able."

"I bet Karen is hoping she doesn't have to deliver this one," Peter laughed.

Fletcher laughed too, "But she has all that experience now. No use letting it goes to waste."

"I've got to tell you something. Last night when Karen and I went to our bedroom, Mama was standing by the window. It's fair to say she heard something, if not all of our discussion last night."

"Oh man. What are we going to do now?" Fletcher's heart sank.

"We go ahead with our story. If you think about it, it gives them a chance to save face too, when they get to Virginia."

"Well, that's right. They won't have to worry about everyone talking about them and looking down on us all." Fletcher conceded.

"Fletcher, our mother is the nosiest person I know. I don't know why we ever thought we could keep a secret from her. Even so, she loves us all dearly and only wants the best for us."

"You are right about that. I say you and Karen make the announcement that you are going to have a baby and Rachel is staying to help out."

"Let's head back; we have a train to catch in Pennsylvania. You and the ladies have to find a place to live. It would be great if you could work out something and continue to stay here."

"That's what Karen and I thought too. We could let Rachel and Dotty have the bedroom downstairs and we could take the upper room. We wouldn't want to risk her falling on those stairs."

They were back at the house. The two brothers' eyes met conspiratorially. "Well," Fletcher said, "here goes. Let's get everyone to breakfast and we'll talk to Mama and Papa afterwards."

They sat around the big boarding house style table and enjoyed a delicious breakfast with hot biscuits, sausage all covered with a peppery, white gravy. Fletcher and Peter loved it and requested more. Rachel and Karen picked at their biscuits. The women were both nervous about telling Mama and Papa about their plans.

After their last cup of coffee, Peter stood and pulled Karen up by his side. Clearing his throat, he started. "Karen and I have a big announcement this morning."

He looked at Karen and she blurted out, "We are going to have a baby!"

Mama and Papa looked surprised. "But dear, I thought the doctor said it would be dangerous for you to have a baby."

Peter said, "That brings us to the second part of our news. Rachel has agreed to stay and help Karen with the delivery."

"Rachel, how can you do that?" Mama asked. "You have a family of your own to take care of! And you and Fletcher have been apart for so long. Do you think it's wise to do this?"

"Karen needs my help. She has been so good to me after what I went through. I want to stay and help her."

Fletcher interjected, "Mama, this won't be easy for any of us. I'm hoping you and Papa will help me with the boys once we get to Virginia. Dotty will stay with her Mommy."

"I don't know what to say," Mama said.

"I'm looking forward to your home cooking, Mama. Mrs. Henderson does alright, but she can't hold a candle to your cooking."

Peter spoke up, "Of course, I'm staying with the women. We are going to try to see if we can work out a plan to stay here at this house. I will find a job and Fletcher will send us a little money to help out with expenses for Rachel and Dotty."

Papa said, "Well, it sounds like the four of you have it all worked out. Mama and I will help anyway we can. But, wouldn't it be better to leave Mama and me here and let Rachel return with her family?"

"We think this is the best way to do this. Rachel still needs time to get over what happened to her, Mama. She still bursts into tears when her mind goes back to that night," Fletcher explained.

Fletcher looked at the faces around the table, each adjusting to the news in their own way. His eyes fell on Joseph and Arwood's faces. They looked like they were ready to cry. The little brothers were tightly holding hands.

"Mommy, you aren't coming to Virginia with us?" said Joseph.

Rachel handed the baby to Karen and went to her sons. She positioned herself between them with her arms around them.

"I can't right now, babies. I have to stay and help Aunt Karen. You're going to have Daddy, Mama and Papa to take care of you. I'm going to miss you both terribly, but don't worry, the time will quickly go by."

Peter piped up, "When we come down in the spring, you will have a new little cousin to play with."

Karen said, "What do you think we will have, a boy or a girl? Which one do you boys want?"

"A boy," said Joseph.

"A girl, then she can play with Dotty," said Arwood.

"Well, let's see who is right! Come over here and give me a hug. I hope whichever one we have, it is as sweet as you two," said Aunt Karen.

They slowly walked over and gave her a halfhearted hug. They were going to miss their Mommy. They didn't understand why she couldn't come with them. Aunt Karen was a grown up, she didn't need their Mommy as much as they did.

CHAPTER 32

Virginia Bound

There are many plans in a man's heart, Nevertheless the LORD's counsel—that will stand.

Proverbs 19:21

Fletcher hired a wagon driver and horses to take them from Lower Manhattan to the train depot in Pennsylvania. He and his family spent a night on the road at a small inn with everyone sharing a single room. He gave his parents the bed and he and the boys camped out on the floor on the two blankets Rachel packed. The children thought this was a great adventure having daddy sleep on the floor with them.

Early the next morning, after a light breakfast, the family traveled on. Joseph and Arwood were so excited to see the big train rolling into the station. They were like bouncing balls on the platform. Fletcher had his work cut out for him trying to hold onto them.

"Daddy, is this the train you rode on?" Joseph asked.

"Yes it is son, and man, does it move fast!"

Arwood seemed frightened by the big steaming monster once it got a little closer. He clung to Fletcher's leg. Fletcher had to carry him on board. Arwood stuck to him like glue for the first hour or so. After that, he was on the seat with Joseph looking out the window at this new world rolling by.

Mama and Papa seemed to enjoy the train ride. Later that evening, they arrived in Roanoke. They were all hungry. Fletcher found a little café that served soup and sandwiches. There was a small motel near the railroad station so they found another room to share so everyone could rest up.

The next morning, Fletcher treated everyone to a hearty breakfast at a nearby diner. With some of the excitement dying out, the little boys became homesick for their mother.

Arwood whined, "Daddy, when is Mommy coming to stay with us?"

"It won't be for awhile, Arwood, but don't worry, I'm going to take good care of you, and so will your Mama and Papa." said Fletcher.

To distract them, Mama spoke up, "Arwood, would you and Joseph like to hear some stories about your Daddy when he was about your age?"

The two boys nodded their heads and looked at their Daddy. It was hard to believe he used to be a little boy like them.

"I do, Mama," said Joseph.

"I'll tell you a story as soon as we get on the last train. Arwood, you know what? I don't think I've had a hug from either one of you this whole morning," said Mama.

Both boys scrambled over and hugged Mama tightly. She loved every minute of it even though they nearly knocked off her glasses in the process. She laughed and hugged them both in return. They really were precious grandchildren.

They boarded the train, *The Huckleberry*, which would carry them all to Blacksburg. It was so named because it was rumored to go so slow that once you reached Blacksburg, you could hop off, pick some huckleberries and jump back on again. The boys thought that would be fun. Fletcher told them no, they had to stay on the train.

What a difference a day made for a child, Fletcher thought. Arwood was eager to go this time. Yesterday, scared to death and clinging to his daddy and today, running ahead to beat his brother getting on board.

Fletcher's mother asked him to sit and talk with her for a spell. He felt apprehensive.

She started, "Fletcher is there anything you want to tell me?"

"Not really Mama. Rachel and I discussed everything to death and then we asked Peter and Karen to discuss it with us. So actually, I'm sick of talking about our situation."

"Son, I worry that you are holding too much inside you. That's not good for you."

"Mama, can we just agree that what happened to Rachel was horrible. That is not something I can get over quickly. I love her and I can see that she is in pain right now."

"Well, I think it's bittersweet that Karen is expecting a baby now after Rachel had such a terrible thing happen to her."

"Mama, we need to be happy for Karen and Peter. Rachel needs this time to heal. The timing actually works out perfectly, don't you think?"

"I don't know what to think," Mama said primly. "She belongs in Virginia with her family."

Fletcher gave a small shrug. "That's what would be easier for the rest of us. I don't think that would be best for Rachel at this time."

H would miss having Rachel at his side. It was now a case of so close, yet so far away too. It was just impossible right now. He looked over at his two boys. The methodical sound of the wheels sliding on the rails put the boys to sleep.

Mama went back to her stitching and kept her thoughts to herself as the slow train climbed the mountain towards Blacksburg. His Papa just looked out the window. Fletcher knew his father couldn't stand a confrontation. So, he usually just kept himself preoccupied with something else.

It was a hot day and the windows were open. Fletcher breathed in the fresh mountain air. Soon, he'd be back in that hole in the earth, hammering out coal and wishing he had all this fresh air to enjoy.

Fletcher thought, back at the camp, everyone probably envied him for being away on a vacation. While it was a break from the monotony of the daily grind, what he had just gone through was no vacation.

The train finally got to Blacksburg. They walked over to the general store and picked up the items they needed to set up their own place.

Fletcher proudly introduced his family to the owners of the store, Bert and Eloise Tilley. They were happy to see his family with him. Both remembered how homesick he had been when they first met him this past winter. His mother didn't need any help putting together her list of groceries. She had Fletcher and his father follow her around with a sack and gathered everything she thought they might need. He was surprised at the amount of food she bought.

Mama just clucked her tongue. "You have to remember, we don't have the garden or canned food reserves we had in the old country. We'll need more store bought groceries until we can get settled."

The men loaded the items into the wagon and young Johnny gave them a ride to their new home. His mother said this time was no charge to thank them for their nice order. He wasn't nearly as talkative as he had been with Fletcher that first time when they met. He listened to the soft German dialect Fletcher spoke with his family. He didn't know what they were saying, but Fletcher's mother seemed pretty bossy, almost as bad as his own mother.

It amazed Johnny that these families coming to his hometown could speak his language, but he couldn't understand a thing they were saying. They must be pretty smart to know two languages, he thought.

When they arrived at the German camp, the men set about getting the two tents set up. Fletcher and the boys would have one and the grandparents the other. The new tents were a couple tents down from Paul Conner's family and their relative, Anna-Leigh. She still tried to catch Fletcher's eye whenever she could and went out of her way to bump into him, to his annoyance.

It would be nice for his sons to have Paul's two boys to play with. Before he left for New York to pick up his family, Fletcher heard that Paul and Helen were expecting their third child. Maybe, that would keep Anna-Leigh occupied, helping her sister with the new baby.

It was Saturday, so several of the men came over to give them a hand and meet Fletcher's family. David held back and took note that Fletcher's wife wasn't with them. He still harbored jealously because Anna-Leigh obviously was interested in Fletcher. He wanted her to notice him, not some married man. She seemed to appreciate his attention while Fletcher was away, but now, he could see once again, she seemed to only have eyes for Fletcher. Where was his wife anyway? David thought that would put an end to Anna-Leigh's infatuation.

The four little boys struck up an instant friendship and were off to explore the creek together. That suited Fletcher just fine since he had work to do. He watched the children racing across the field. It was good to have his boys here with him.

Mama was like an army general barking out orders. Fletcher and everyone else just did whatever she told them. Everything was organized in no time. She invited all the helpers back on Sunday afternoon for a pot of her homemade stew. Fletcher thanked them for their help.

He decided to walk down towards the creek and check on the boys. When he got there, he was surprised to find Anna-Leigh with them.

"Oh, hello Fletcher," she said, coming over to him. "I thought I would make sure the boys were getting along."

Fletcher wished there was some way to just graciously get away without having to have a civil conversation. He had noticed that she didn't normally seem to be much help to her sister with the two children, but now that his boys were here, she took an interest.

"Thank you; I was doing the same thing. I'll keep an eye on them all so you can go back now."

"There's no rush. I want to talk with you for a bit."

Fletcher could barely conceal his grimace. "I've got a lot to do, Anna-Leigh."

Anna-Leigh eyed him curiously. He seemed nervous to her. "Fletcher, I didn't see your wife. I was looking forward to meeting her."

There it was. This woman was relentless in her pursuit. She'd make a good hunter, but he wasn't game. "She will be joining us soon. My brother and sister-in-law are expecting a child. Rachel is staying with them in New York until the baby arrives."

"How long will that be?" Anna-Leigh seemed unusually interested.

"I don't know exactly, as long as it takes, I guess."

"I can't believe she would stay and leave you with all the responsibility of the children, as hard as you work."

"Well believe it or not, Rachel and I are in complete agreement about the matter. My parents are all the help I need. Good day, Anna-Leigh."

Fletcher called to his boys. They were having too much fun; they just waved and went back to playing with their new friends.

Anna-Leigh watched his retreating back and smiled to herself. This might be her chance. She was not beyond using the children as an excuse to get close to Fletcher. He was a man, after all. He would get lonely eventually and when he did, she would be right there to cheer him up.

Funny how things seemed to be lining up for the two of them, she thought. She'd heard talk of something called karma. This had to be it.

CHAPTER 33

Making a Home

The plans of the diligent lead surely to plenty, But those of everyone who is hasty, surely to poverty.

Proverbs 21:5

Fletcher and his father began to explore available home sites in earnest. The perfect land as far as they were concerned would be closer to the river for fishing, have woods and mountains for hunting, gently rolling land with open pasture for their family homes, garden and livestock. A tall order at any price, Fletcher thought. It occurred to him that they were trying to recreate their old family farm here in Virginia. Of course, that was the work generations of his family had done. He probably shouldn't have expected any less.

They explored the acreage right by the river, but worried about flooding and there simply wasn't enough useful farmland.

They finally settled on some land in the community of Long Shop. They liked the idea of already having some business around them such as the blacksmith shop and grist mill. They had to maintain some reserve cash to build their homes so price per acre was a real consideration.

Fletcher and his Poppa learned that Sam Blackwell wasn't in good health and was raising seven children. It was said that he and his wife struggled to eke out a living. Neighbors had said they thought he might sell off a little land.

Sam heard the knock at his door and saw two Germans standing on his porch, an older gentleman and a young man.

"Yes, what can I do for you?" he asked.

John spoke up. "We want to talk to you about buying some of your land. Are you interested in selling any land?"

"I'm not sure whether I am or not, but I heard you fellows have been asking around about some land. Let's sit out here on the porch and talk a spell," said Sam. "This September is turning into an Indian summer, I do believe." He turned back inside and called out, "Jane, can you get us some cold water to drink?"

John and Fletcher watched the children running around the yard, chasing one another, laughing like they didn't have a care in the world. They screamed and hooted as someone was tagged.

"How much land do you figure you need?" Sam asked.

"We could make do with fifty acres, but would prefer to have a hundred," John told him.

"What do you plan to do with the land?" Sam inquired.

"We would like to build a house we could all live in at first and then, build individual houses for my two sons and their families sometime down the road," said John. "We are farmers by trade. This looks like good rich soil."

"Yes, it has served us well. My health isn't so good, but we have all these children to help us with the garden. We just manage to grow enough to feed our family," said Sam.

Jane arrived with a metal pail with a dipper hanging on it, some cold water from their well and a few glasses for the men. The men served themselves and thanked her. The water was delicious.

Sam said, "Jane, sit with us for a minute. These men want to buy some land off of us."

Jane looked exhausted. Her apron and the front of her dress were wet from doing laundry. She yelled to the children, "Aubrey, Sharon, take the kids around back and play so we can hear ourselves talk."

The youngest little girl who appeared to be about three came and climbed upon her mother's lap. She grinned at Fletcher.

John said, "How are you, ma'am?

"Tired," she responded. "These young'uns keep me plenty busy. The older ones are a big help, though."

Sam said, "We own about a hundred and twenty five acres counting the land the house sits on. Of course, a lot of it is wooded and there's some good hunting in those woods. We see deer, turkey, squirrel, even an occasional bear. I can't get after it like I used to."

"We are prepared to offer you twenty five dollars an acre," said John. Even that amount would stretch John's budget, but above all he wanted to be fair.

Twenty five hundred dollars was a great deal of money and would mean some easier times for him and his family, Sam thought.

"Jane and I have talked about selling out and moving to West Virginia to be closer to some of our family," said John. "How much would you be willing to offer me for the whole part and parcel including the house?"

"Do you mind if we take a look at the house?" said John. "We don't mean to intrude, ma'am, but we would need to see it to know how much it is worth to us."

"You are welcome to come inside," said Jane. "It's laundry day, so it's not as clean as usual. I believe in keeping up my house."

The men rose and Jane and Sam walked them through their home. About three children followed them and Jane was carrying the littlest one on her hip.

Fletcher and his Poppa didn't know what to expect, but the woman's home was spotless. Everything was in its place except for little piles of laundry. Supper was cooking. The main floor had a nice size living area with a large eat-in kitchen with a long, hand hewn table with benches on both sides and a chair at either end. There was a parlor and a good sized bedroom, one bathroom. Upstairs, they found four bedrooms with closets in each one. The house had a nice root cellar, dirt floored basement with a door leading to the backyard.

"You have a nice home here, Sam," said John. "We'd love to have it, but I'm not sure we can afford it."

"We would sell it all for four thousand," said Sam.

"That sounds fair," said John. "How soon could you be out?"

"Have you got that kind of money?" asked Sam, in surprise.

"It is more than we'd intended to spend, but we can get that much money," said John.

"Well, I think you just bought yourself a farm. We'll need a couple of months to get ourselves packed and moved to West Virginia. How about if we settle up around the end of November? That way, you can celebrate Christmas here," said Sam.

"My son and I will contact a lawyer and have the papers drawn up. Do you need a deposit?" asked John.

"No deposit needed. How about if we just shake on it? We call that a gentleman's agreement around here," said Sam.

The two older men shook hands. Fletcher and John said goodbye. Fletcher saw tears in Jane's eyes and the children following them around were quizzing her about what was going on.

Fletcher and John got back into the wagon. John had bought the two horses and wagon right after getting to the area. He didn't like being dependent on others to get him to town or wherever he had to go. Father and son discussed the transaction all the way back home.

Hilda was standing in the yard making lye soap over the cook fire when she saw them approaching from afar. They both looked like the cat that swallowed the canary she thought. She could see them carrying on an animated conversation. They grew quiet as they approached her.

"Well, don't keep me in suspense," she said. "How did it go? Are we going to get the land?"

"Well, yes, but-"John started.

"You had to pay more for it then you expected, right?" Hilda interrupted.

"Well, yes and no," said Fletcher.

"For heaven's sake, will one of you tell me how much our new home site is going to cost us?" an exasperated Hilda exclaimed.

John took her in his arms and danced her around in a circle, laughing at her sputtering face. "My dear, we are buying a hundred and twenty five acres and they are throwing in their five bedroom house too."

"Now, John, can we afford that?" Hilda said breathlessly, "And quit spinning me around. You are making me dizzy!"

"We certainly can, but will have to be very frugal to make ends meet. Fletcher will have his job at the mines to help the family out for a while," said John. "But not having to build a home right away means we can concentrate on our farm and get a faster start!"

Fletcher smiled watching his parents celebrating the purchase. He was so glad to have them here with him and was glad they had something to be happy about.

"Well, I'm going to write to Peter and Karen, and Rachel to let them know the good news," said Hilda.

The time flew by and the week before Thanksgiving, they took possession of their new home. Jane Blackwell had left it in spotless condition, but that didn't keep Hilda from cleaning it thoroughly from top to bottom. Fletcher thought that must be how his momma claimed her space.

John and Hilda took the bedroom on the main floor. Fletcher took one of the bedrooms upstairs and put the boys in one of the other 3 rooms. Karen and Rachel could have one of the bedrooms as a nursery to share, what a luxury, thought Fletcher.

Fletcher's parents hired Clyde to build their beds, kitchen table, benches and chairs. Clyde had done well with his furniture trade. He was able to put back some money. If all went well he would be able to bring his family over in the summer of 1921. And although he'd never tell anyone, especially not Mr. Henderson, his dream was to have a furniture shop in town soon.

CHAPTER 34

Homecoming

Who can find a virtuous wife? For her worth is far above rubies.

Proverbs 31:10

Over the long months of Rachel, Karen and Peter being away, there had been countless letters back and forth from Rachel to Fletcher and the children, and John and Hilda to them.

The Christmas holiday was especially hard for them all being apart from each other. Hilda begged John to take her and the children to New York to visit with them. John flatly turned down her request. He reminded her that they were fortunate to have the nice home they were in, but that their money was tight. They still needed to buy all the seedlings for a garden, repair and add more fencing, build more sheds, the list droned on.

They put up a Christmas tree for the children in the nice large parlor. Rachel had her mother's decorations with her so the tree was sparsely decorated. The boys helped string popcorn and made red berry garland. Hilda missed her Christmas tree candles, but they couldn't bring everything with them. Still the tree was beautiful in its simplicity. She got candy canes at the hardware store and some green and red plaid ribbon and fashioned bright little bows to adorn the tree. She baked cookies and candy, made hot chocolate and they all sang Christmas carols together.

Fletcher had Clyde make the boys a little wooden train set and a set of wooden croquet mallets and balls for their Christmas gifts. He and his Poppa painted the wooden crafted toys. The boys were thrilled with their gifts.

Fletcher had bought Rachel and Karen both a scarf and an ornate clip to go in their hair. He sent Rachel a small bottle of perfume with a little atomizer. The glass bottle was a beautiful deep rose hue. He wrote her a very personal letter telling her how much he loved and missed her. He got his brother a nice pair of store bought leather gloves. It took two to three weeks for the mail delivery which was so much better than the oceanic delivery time.

Rachel was having an easy pregnancy this time around. She had not gained much weight, but the doctor in New York assured her the baby was healthy. She had framed the pictures the photographer brought to their apartment. That was her gift to them all. The postage was too great to mail them, so she would bring them when they all came down in the Spring. She assured the family that the pictures had turned out wonderful. They were a family treasure.

It seemed like they had just packed up Christmas when the first robin was setting up a nest on their front porch. Looking out the doors and windows, all Fletcher saw was leafless trees, gray grass and an occasional hard frost. Then, his dad started pointing out the perennial sprouts popping through the earth, the tiny buds on the trees. Mother Earth knew Spring was on the way whether they were paying attention or not.

On March 23, 1921, a robust baby boy was born in a boarding house in lower Manhattan. He was long and skinny with light blonde hair. Karen had gotten a recipe for a syrup laced baby formula from the owner of the boarding house and the baby boy sucked the nipple on the baby bottle like it was the best thing in the world.

Peter and Karen had been putting back little items for the baby all along. Peter was so proud of having a son. They named him Andrew. He could easily pass as their own with his golden shock of hair and blue eyes.

Rachel was surprised that she didn't harbor any ill will towards the child. He was precious and beautiful. She thanked God for the easy labor.

They completed the necessary adoption paperwork and filed it in the city offices. Rachel had cried when her name was listed as the mother and "unknown" was placed in the space for the father. What did it matter? Who would ever see the paperwork? They would be living in another state as soon as Rachel was able to travel. It was just a formality. Peter folded up their copy of the paperwork and placed it inside a tear in the lining of his valise. No one else needed to see this document.

A month later, they packed up a wagon and followed a similar course of travel as Fletcher had taken with his family when they travelled home last summer. Rachel felt her strength return and something else, a sense of joy and expectation. She wanted to see her big boys.

Dotty was not walking, but running and getting into everything. She was a delightful child. Having Dotty here with her kept Rachel from becoming too dissatisfied with their predicament. Soon, they would be a real family again. Funny how you take that for granted sometimes, but how important it is.

She loved watching Karen and Peter with baby Andrew. Karen seemed to be blooming before their eyes. Peter thought she was more beautiful than ever with the precious child in her arms. He felt a little awkward still when handling the baby. Andrew was so tiny, he worried he would hurt him with his big, clumsy hands.

No baby could be loved as much by anyone as Andrew was by his new found parents. Rachel rarely held him. She didn't want to interfere with that all important bond that was forming so naturally between the child and his parents. Karen was a natural mother, so patient and gentle. She would fall asleep herself rocking Andrew to sleep.

Fletcher and the boys were going to take the train and meet them in Roanoke. His father was going to meet them with the wagon in Blacksburg when they arrived. He couldn't wait to show them their new home. He thanked God for providing the perfect house for them all.

Peter and his family and Rachel arrived in Roanoke on a beautiful clear day. The lay of the land reminded Peter of Germany. He liked all the commerce that surrounded the railroad station. He got their bags and looked about. There was Fletcher and the boys running towards them.

"Mommy, Mommy, here we are," shouted Joseph. He threw his arms around her and kissed her cheek so hard.

Arwood was right on Joseph's heels. Rachel hugged and kissed him. She looked past them to Fletcher. She searched his face, took in his big smile and misty eyes.

"Hello, Rachel," Fletcher said and put his arm around her and kissed the top of her head. She was bent down talking to the boys.

He took Dotty from her arms and tossed her up in the air. She giggled and squealed in delight. He worried that his little girl would be afraid of him. They hadn't had much time to get to know each other. It thrilled him that she seemed so happy, go lucky.

"Here, Joseph," Fletcher said. "You and Arwood hold onto your little sister's hand and walk over to that bench while I help Uncle Peter with the suitcases."

They did as he instructed. Dotty pulled to get away, so Joseph picked her up and carried her.

Fletcher turned back to Rachel. He saw more of those tears of joy glistening in her eyes. He took her in his arms and kissed her soundly. "I've missed you so much, sweetheart. I'm so glad you're home with me. I don't ever want to be away from you again."

Rachel leaned her head against her husband as they walked over to where the children were playing. Dotty was trying her best to get down and run around. Joseph was holding on for dear life. Arwood was tickling her and making her laugh. They were so sweet together.

Fletcher went over to speak to Karen. Something looked so different about her, he didn't know what it was, but she certainly looked happy. He looked at the little bundle in her arms. Her eyes seemed to be begging him to love their baby.

"Well, who do we have here, Karen?" Fletcher asked.

"This is Andrew Broce, the apple of his Daddy's eye." Karen said.

When she pulled the blanket back to let Fletcher see him, Andrew's little eyes flew open. Fletcher's breath caught. He looked just like Peter! No one would ever suspect that he was not their biological child.

Fletcher held out his little finger and felt Andrew's tight baby grip. "Can I hold him, Karen?"

She smiled gratefully and handed the baby over. It had been a long time since Fletcher had held a baby as small as Andrew. He seemed so helpless and sweet. His heart caught, to think he had wanted Rachel to get rid of this child before he was born. Bless her heart for insisting that he live. Only God could produce something as precious as a child.

He handed Andrew back to his mother. Yes, Karen was his mother and Peter was his father. That felt so right to Fletcher.

Rachel was holding Dotty with both of their boys hanging onto the skirt of her dress. She'd been watching Fletcher with baby Andrew, wondering what his reaction would be. *It's going to be alright, she thought.*

The two families had just enough time to grab some lunch before boarding the train to Blacksburg. Fletcher told them all more details about the land and house Papa and Mama had bought.

"It sounds perfect for our growing family, Fletcher," Peter exclaimed.

"You better enjoy the break you're having right now, because Papa has got a list a mile long of jobs for the two of us when we get back," said Fletcher.

Peter laughed. "Well, it will be like old times all of us working together again. Will you stay on at the mines?"

"I'll have to so we can save up to build our own place someday. Man, it is good to have you and Karen here with us," said Fletcher slapping his brother on the back.

"I've had enough of city life. I can't wait to get out there hunting and fishing with you and Papa," said Peter. The men launched into a long discussion about the variety of game and where the best fishing hole was.

Karen and Rachel were talking about making curtains for the nursery and bedrooms. How would three women share a house and especially a kitchen, they wondered.

Karen laughed, "I'm ok with letting Momma do all the cooking, how about you Rachel?"

"Hmmm, you might have something there, Karen," Rachel laughed.

Edwards Brothers Malloy
Thorofare, NJ USA
October 28, 2014